SENT AWAY

SENT AWAY

Jonathan Croall

Oxford University Press
Oxford New York Melbourne

Oxford University Press, Walton Street,
Oxford OX2 6DP

*Oxford New York Toronto
Delhi Bombay Calcutta Madras Karachi
Petaling Jaya Singapore Hong Kong Tokyo
Nairobi Dar es Salaam Cape Town
Melbourne Auckland*

and associated companies in
Berlin Ibadan

Oxford is a trade mark of Oxford University Press

A CIP catalogue record for this book is available
from the British Library

ISBN 0 19 271657 3

Typeset by Pentacor PLC, High Wycombe, Bucks
Printed in
Great Britain

Other books by Jonathan Croall

Don't Shoot the Goalkeeper
(OUP)

The Parents' Day School Book
(Panther)

Neill of Summerhill: The Permanent Rebel
(Routledge)

All the Best, Neill: Letters from Summerhill
(Deutsch)

Don't You Know There's A War On?:
The People's Voice 1939–1945
(Hutchinson)

Dig for History: Active Learning
Across the Curriculum
(Southgate)

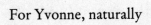

For Yvonne, naturally

Contents

Author's Note

This story is based on the real-life experiences of hundreds of boys and girls who were sent out to Australia, Canada, and South Africa in the earlier part of this century. Many of their stories are told in the book *Lost Children of the Empire* by Philip Bean and Joy Melville, published by Unwin Hyman in 1989, and in the documentary film of the same name, made by Domino Films in the same year.

While Joe and Ellen are fictitious characters, their story is typical of what happened to many boys and girls of their age during these years. Some of the children had an easier time of it; others, unfortunately, suffered much greater hardship, in ways that affected them for the rest of their lives.

Chapter 1

BREAKING UP

Something was wrong. Ellen and Joe had known it for some time. They'd kept their worries to themselves. But now it seemed to be getting worse.

Ellen had heard the arguments all week. Why does Mum get so angry with him, she thought, as she lay in bed, listening to the rise and fall of her voice? I'm sure Dad's not done anything wrong. She was tempted to go out on the landing and listen. Once she got as far as her bedroom door, but thought better of it. It's better not to, she told herself firmly, climbing back into bed. It's private really.

She remembered again that afternoon during the war, before they were evacuated, when Dad had come home from hospital, after he'd been wounded in the head helping to get people out of their bombed houses. From that day onwards, Dad had seemed a different man. Before, he had been full of fun and life, noisy, bursting with ideas, always wanting to go places. Now he was silent and serious. He seemed to live in a world of his own, almost as if she and Joe were no longer his children.

Joe had also heard the loud voices. For several mornings now he had noticed his mother's red-rimmed eyes beneath her dark, wavy hair, and the paleness of her pretty, round face as she moved about the kitchen.

He also realized that Dad was going to work earlier. Perhaps, Joe decided, he's got more to do in the park at the moment? He thought of the piles of brown and gold leaves that he and Ellen had shuffled through recently. He remembered Dad talking about the large new flower-beds he and the other gardeners were making by the riverside.

1

Yes, that's why he has his breakfast before me, Joe told himself, as he turned over in his bed.

The next day was the last before half-term. Ellen would be glad of the break, for school had been harder this term. Before, in all the muddle and sadness of wartime, the teachers had been kind and friendly, and had not been too worried about work being done on time, or whether you brought your gas mask to school. But now, especially since two teachers who had been in the army had come back, everyone suddenly seemed more strict again.

One of them, Mr Baker, who taught geography, really annoyed Ellen. He liked to make fun of the slower children, and when she tried to help one girl with a map, he made her stay in during break, and write out 'I Will Mind My Own Business' a hundred times. Previously geography had been her favourite subject; now she wasn't so sure.

One thing had changed for the better, though: now that Joe was eleven, *he* was in the senior school too. Ellen didn't see much of him during the day, except in the playground. Sometimes, if no one was looking, he would wave at her. She knew how shy and uncertain of himself he was, and how much he depended upon her, even though there wasn't much more than a year between them. So she kept her eyes open, in case he got bullied by any of the older children.

At first Joe had felt lost in the bigger school. The playground seemed enormous, and only two of his friends from the junior school had come here with him. So he was glad Ellen was around, even if he usually only saw her in the distance with her friends. It was good to know he could go to her if anything went wrong—as he had so often done at home.

At the end of the afternoon, when the final bell went, the children jostled noisily into the street, calling out to each other as they split up.

2

'Going to Chelsea tomorrow?'

'We can't, stupid, they're away.'

'Don't forget to bring my scarf, Linda.'

'I won't. I'll come after tea.'

'Hey, Tony, want to come to the fleapit tomorrow?'

'My Dad's already taking me.'

They spread out eagerly through the Battersea streets in groups of two or three. As it was a warm day, Ellen and Joe took the long way home. They stopped to watch some younger children playing on the bomb site next to the church. Ellen noticed two small boys digging in the earth.

'Joe.'

'Yes.'

'Can you remember the children who lived here before the war?'

'No. But they must be dead, mustn't they?'

'That depends. They might have been vaccies.'

'I suppose so.'

She thought for a moment. 'I really miss Wales sometimes.'

'Me too. Do you think we'll ever go back?'

'Shouldn't think so.'

'Maybe Mum and Dad would take us for a holiday there?'

'Maybe.'

'We could swim in that lake and catch fish again!'

'Yes.'

'And go for pony rides across the valley.'

'Yes, that was fun.'

Joe was excited now. 'Let's ask them, shall we?'

'What now?'

'Yes.'

'All right.'

'Race you back.'

They ran along the street, weaving in and out of the women queuing outside the shops in the sunshine. Ellen wondered when all this queuing would stop. It seemed strange that you still had to bring your ration book along and wait for ages, even though the war had been over for several months.

They reached the end of their road, with Joe just ahead of Ellen—he was pleased he could do at least one thing better than her.

'Let's go in the back way,' he said, trying to get his breath back. 'Dad'll be home by now.'

'All right,' Ellen said, between gasps.

They made their way round to the back of the terrace, and along the narrow, unpaved path between the two rows of gardens. Joe swung his satchel cheerfully, scaring a large tortoise shell cat off the wall. They reached their back gate, and Ellen peered through the gap in the wooden slats.

'What can you see?' Joe asked, wishing he was taller.

'Dad's there all right,' Ellen said. 'I can see his bike by the wall. Let's go as far as the shelter.'

She opened the gate. The two of them walked cautiously through the well-kept garden, until they reached the Anderson shelter. Ellen thought again about the nights they had spent there during the bombing at the beginning of the war, before they were evacuated. She remembered the fear, and the terrible cold, and the hunger during the long raids. But she also remembered the excitement, the feeling of adventure as you packed up your rations in case the siren went, the reading by candlelight, and the wondering what sort of world you would wake up to in the morning.

'I think I can hear Dad in the sitting-room,' said Joe, interrupting her thoughts. 'Let's surprise him.'

'All right,' Ellen replied, her mind still on the war. How long ago it seemed!

Crouching, Ellen and Joe moved to below the sitting-room window. Slowly they raised their heads above the window-sill, and looked inside. They saw Dad, still in his work overalls, facing them at the other end of the room.

Opposite him was a woman. She was talking to him, using her hands a lot, while Dad stood there, nodding now and then.

Then they realized Dad was crying. As the sunlight poured into the room, they could see tears on his face. They looked at each other. Neither of them had ever seen him cry before, and it seemed all wrong.

They crouched down out of sight, and crept back to the Anderson shelter. Joe gazed up anxiously at Ellen.

'What's the matter with Dad?' he asked.

'How should I know?' said Ellen sharply, trying to hide her fear.

What she did know was that something terrible had happened, something she felt sure was to do with Mum. She stood uncertainly for a moment, leaning against the iron side of the shelter. The sky was cloudless, they had a week off school—surely everything wasn't going to be spoilt now?

'I think we should go round the front,' she said finally. 'Come on.'

Joe followed, accepting her decision about what was best, as he always did. He was puzzled and upset by what he had seen. He was used to his mother crying—though it often pained him, it didn't surprise him. But Dad . . . ! Usually he just went quiet if he was unhappy, or found something to do in the garden. Joe wished he were able to do the same—instead of getting tearful, and then being teased by other children. But now Dad was behaving more like Mum. Joe felt confused.

They reached the front door, and stood on the step, listening for voices inside. Everything seemed quiet. They pressed their noses to the frosted glass, but could see nothing. Ellen took out her key, and opened the door. They dropped their satchels in the narrow hall. The sitting-room door opened, and the woman they had seen through the window came out. She was wearing a pink cardigan, and her hair was in a bun.

'Hello, children,' she said cheerfully. 'Come on in.' They walked past her into the room. It was empty.

'I don't suppose you remember your Aunty Muriel, do you?' She smiled. 'I hardly recognize you myself. You're both so grown-up now.'

'Where's Dad?' Joe asked.

'What? Oh, he's upstairs in the . . . bathroom.' She moved towards the door, taking her smile with her. 'Now, why don't the two of you just sit here, and I'll go—'

'Why is he upset?' Ellen asked.

Aunty Muriel stopped. Ellen wondered why this bossy, interfering woman smiled so much, especially when Dad was upset.

'What makes you think . . .?' Aunty Muriel began.

'We were in the garden,' Ellen said impatiently.

'Oh. I see.' The smile turned down a little at the sides. 'Well, my dears, I'm afraid . . .' She stopped, and looked towards the door. 'Just a moment.' She stepped into the hall, and the children heard her call upstairs.

'Sam, are you there? The children are back from school.'

Ellen and Joe listened for a reply, but none came. Then they heard Dad coming slowly down the stairs. There was a short, whispered conversation in the hall. Then he came in, followed by Aunty Muriel, still smiling faintly.

'Hello, you two,' Dad said. He put an arm each round their shoulders, and led them to the sofa. Ellen noticed he had changed into his ordinary clothes. She looked at his long, kindly face, which only a few moments ago had been streaked with tears. She noticed how pale he was, and that he was shaking slightly.

'What's wrong, Dad?' she said quietly. He glanced at her, and she caught a puzzled look in his dark-brown eyes.

'I'll be in the kitchen if you want me, Sam,' Aunty Muriel said, and left the three of them together. There was silence.

Joe remembered the times they had sat before on this sofa, all the stories Dad had read to them when they were younger. He wished it was story time now, and not all these real things happening he couldn't understand.

Dad ran a hand through his fair hair, which Joe saw was even untidier than usual. Then he raised his eyes from the carpet, and spoke slowly. 'I expect you're wondering why Muriel's here. The fact is . . .' He hesitated. 'It's like this, you see. Mum and I haven't been getting on very well recently—you've probably noticed. Well, today she decided she wanted to go away for a while, to . . . to think things over. She's gone to Wales. It's all been a bit sudden, she rang Muriel from the station this morning, and asked her—'

He stopped, made as if to get up, and then sank back against the green cushions. Joe leaned against his arm, feeling sick in his stomach, and not knowing what to say. Ellen stared out of the window, trying to understand the meaning of Dad's words.

'Do you mean she's not going to live with us any more?' she asked eventually.

'Oh no, Ellen,' Dad replied quickly. 'She just needs some time to herself, that's all.'

He got up, and walked slowly to the window. Ellen felt bewildered by what Dad had said: how could Mum just leave like that, suddenly, and not even say anything to them? She was angry and hurt.

'I don't understand, why didn't she tell us she was going?' Joe asked.

Dad shook his head. 'I don't know, Joe. There are a lot of things about Mum I don't really understand.'

Ellen saw Joe was on the point of tears. She moved along the sofa, and took his hand. 'We'll help you, Dad, won't we, Joe?'

'Yes,' Joe replied, unhappily.

Dad turned to face them. 'You're good kids. I'm sure we'll manage.'

Ellen had a sudden thought. 'What about Aunty Muriel?' she said.

Dad returned to the sofa. 'She's kindly agreed to stay here for a while, so we can sort ourselves out.'

7

'How long is she going to stay?' Ellen asked, anxiously.

'At least over half term,' Dad replied. 'You see, I've still got to go to work.'

'But, Dad, we're old enough to look after ourselves. Aren't we, Joe?'

'Yes,' Joe said. But he was not at all sure they were. Wasn't that what mothers were supposed to do? He felt very confused. Why had Mum suddenly gone to Wales? Didn't she love Ellen and him any more?

He remembered he had been angry with her last week, because she wouldn't let him go and play in the park until he finished his homework. Was that why she decided to go?

Dad was silent for a moment. 'Perhaps you *are* old enough, in some ways. But I still think we should take up Aunty Muriel's offer.'

'Doesn't she have her own children?' Ellen asked, frowning.

'Yes,' Dad replied. 'Uncle Tom's keeping an eye on them.'

'Dad, why's Mum gone to Wales?' Joe asked.

'Well, Joe,' Dad said, slowly, 'I don't exactly know, but maybe because it has good memories for her. You liked being there too, didn't you?'

Joe suddenly understood. 'Do you mean she's gone back to our cottage and the river and everything?'

Dad put his hands together, fingers and thumbs touching. Joe thought for a moment he was praying. 'Maybe,' he said. 'She didn't actually tell Aunty Muriel whereabouts in Wales she was going. She just said she would phone —'

'Did I hear my name?' said Aunty Muriel, marching in with a tray of tea. 'I thought you might all need some of this, to keep your spirits up.' She placed it noisily on the table by the window.

'I don't like tea,' Joe said.

'I'm not thirsty, thank you,' Ellen added.

Dad got up from the sofa. 'Thank you, Muriel, it's good of you to do this.'

So Aunty Muriel stayed. But Joe and Ellen didn't take to her at all. She bustled around during the day, never keeping still, always with that annoying smile on her face. In the evening she would sit in the old green armchair, doing some darning, or knitting a jersey from a huge ball of purple wool.

Ellen knew her aunt was being helpful: she cooked the meals, and went to the shops most days. I don't want to upset Dad any more, she thought. So she was polite to her, even though she didn't like her. She was always *doing* something. There never seemed to be any time for fun—or even for just talking. Not like Mum, she thought. She remembered all the toy animals she had when she was younger, and how when Dad and Joe were out playing football, Mum would join in, sitting on her bedroom floor and acting out stories with the animals.

Suddenly Ellen wanted to play those games again. She even got down the bag of animals from the top of the cupboard where they had been put away—'For my grandchildren', Mum had said. She looked at the bears and the monkeys, and the large blue hippopotamus; but it wasn't the same.

Normally, Joe was more likely to keep his feelings to himself than Ellen was. But he didn't like the way Aunty Muriel wanted to have everything clean and tidy, especially when it came to his room. Once he came in and found her putting all his toys away in the wrong cupboard.

'Ah, Joe,' she said, 'you really should try to keep your things in order. Then you'll always know where they are, won't you?'

'You're not allowed in my room without permission,' Joe said. He noticed his aunt's silly grin get wider than ever. 'This is *my* room, I don't *want* you in here!' he shouted angrily.

9

For a moment the smile disappeared. 'I don't think that's a very nice way to speak to your aunt,' she said, rising from the floor. 'Especially when I'm doing my best to take care of you now that . . . until your mother comes back.'

Joe sat on his bed, opened a book, and pretended to read it. Aunty Muriel left the room. Joe threw the book on the floor, lay full length on his bed, and stared at the ceiling. I wish Mum would come back *now*, he thought angrily. She would never come into my room like that, or put things in the wrong place.

He was puzzled. Why had Mum and Dad's quarrelling got so much worse? He knew that when the war started Dad had said he wasn't going to fight, that he didn't believe in killing people—that's why he had gone to help in the special ambulance service. He dimly remembered that this had upset Mum and caused a lot of arguments, and more than once Mum had walked out of the house—though she'd soon come back. But since Dad's injury, and his getting the gardening job in Battersea Park, the quarrelling had stopped—until these last few weeks. Why had it all suddenly changed?

Now, during half-term, Dad seemed even quieter than usual. He spent most of his time at home in the garden, digging the vegetable patch or working in the greenhouse.

Once Joe looked out of the window and saw him leaning on his spade, gazing at the fir tree in the next garden. He stood there for several minutes, almost as still as a statue.

In the evenings he didn't say much either. At supper he would ask Joe and Ellen what they'd been up to, then lose interest in what they were saying. Once or twice he would talk about his work: about where they had got to with the new flower-bed, or how one man had got the sack because he got drunk at lunchtime and drove the grass-cutting van into a tree.

But as soon as the meal was over he would go into the sitting-room, turn the radio on, and stay there for most of the evening, listening to the Home Service. Sometimes he would fall asleep, while Aunty Muriel's knitting needles clicked away from the other side of the room. When Joe or Ellen came in to say good-night, she would say: 'Don't wake your father, my dears; he needs to catch up on his shut-eye. Pop along, and I'll come and tuck you up in a few minutes.'

After the first time this happened, Ellen and Joe undressed and got into bed in record time, so they could pretend to be asleep by the time Aunty Muriel came up. In this way they could avoid being kissed, and called 'lambkins', and having to listen to her prayers for them.

The telephone call came on the last evening of half-term. Ellen was alone in the kitchen, staying up late to draw a map of Australia for her geography lesson. Outside the rain was slanting across the window. She picked up the receiver, in her mind still trying to get the shape of Tasmania right.

'Macaulay 5692,' she said.

There was a silence at the other end. Then Ellen knew who it was.

'Is that you, Mum?' she said, suddenly excited.

'Hello, Ellen love,' said a familiar voice. It was wonderful to hear her again!—but Ellen thought she sounded sad.

'Are you all right, Mum?'

'Yes, I'm fine, Ellen. What about you and Joe?'

'We're missing you.'

'I know.' There was a long pause. 'I'm sorry, love. It's hard to explain. I wish . . . what has Dad told you?'

'He said you'd gone to Wales.'

'Did he tell you why?'

'Not really. He said you weren't getting on very well together. When are you coming back, Mum?'

'Well, that's why—' There was a pause. 'Is your Dad there, Ellen? I think perhaps I should talk to him.'

'But why can't you tell *me* what's happening?'

11

'I don't know if you're old enough, love. It's difficult to explain, especially over the phone.'

Ellen took a deep breath. 'Don't you love Dad any more?' she said, clutching the black receiver hard.

There was another short silence. 'It's not that. I shall always love your Dad. But . . . so much has changed, the war has made such a difference to our lives.'

'You mean Dad's injury?'

'Yes. It's made him such a different person—sometimes I hardly recognize him.'

'But he can't help that, Mum.'

'I know, love. I know. Oh it's hard to explain . . . Sometimes I don't know what I'm doing myself . . . things have happened, you see . . . oh, life isn't the same.'

Ellen watched the raindrops slide down the window pane. Her mouth felt dry and strange. 'When are you coming back, Mum?' she said eventually.

'I don't know yet. I'm staying here for a little longer. There's a little hotel near the post office; do you remember it?'

'Yes,' Ellen said, seeing the small whitewashed building. In her mind she saw Mum standing outside, leaning against the wall, staring dreamily out across the valley, her grey-green eyes lost in the landscape.

'It's quiet here, I can go for long walks, and think,' Mum was saying. 'A lot of the time I think of you and Joe, you know.'

'Can we come and see you then?'

'Not for the moment, I think, love.'

'But Mum—'

She stopped, as she realized Dad was in the room.

'Shall I have a word now, Ellen?' he said.

She looked at his unhappy face, said 'Bye, Mum' into the receiver, passed it to Dad, ran up the stairs, and collapsed on her bed in tears.

As they got ready for school the next day, Joe and Ellen were glad to hear Aunty Muriel would be going home the following day. Ellen had found it harder and harder even to be polite to her—she was such a bossy woman, and never seemed to leave you alone. As for Joe, he had had several more quarrels with her—about getting his trousers dirty, about going out to play football in the rain, about the way he held his fork—all things which, Joe kept telling himself, were none of her business.

Neither of them felt able to ask Dad when Mum might come back. Ellen hoped he might say something that morning, after the phone call. But at breakfast he was even quieter than usual, only really noticing her and Joe as they left the table.

After a week of Aunty Muriel, Joe and Ellen were pleased to be back amongst their friends. It was good to hear what other families had been doing. And when they got home again at tea time, even Aunty Muriel seemed almost bearable.

That evening, after the gloomy weather of the previous week, the sky suddenly cleared, and the late evening sun poured into the garden. Dad had taken a chair out on to the small square of grass in the middle. Ellen, seeing him through the window, suddenly felt she wanted to join him. She came out and knelt on the grass beside his chair. She watched a blackbird land on the fence nearby, and enjoyed for a moment the feel of the warm air.

She noticed Dad's eyes were closed. 'Hello, Dad,' she said.

'Hello, love,' he replied, without opening them.

'Dad, what did Mum say last night? Is she coming home?'

His eyes slowly opened. He looked down at her. 'Not yet, Ellen. She needs more time to herself.'

'Time for what?'

'Just to think, love.'

'But why does she have to go to Wales to do that?'

He was silent. Ellen saw the blackbird swoop off the fence and land in the flower bed.

When Dad spoke, she noticed how quiet his voice was. 'Sometimes you can see things more clearly if you're somewhere different, away from people.'

Ellen thought she could understand this. 'But don't you mind her going, Dad?'

'I miss her very much, yes. But I have to be patient, Ellen. We all of us have to be.'

He closed his eyes once more. She watched as the blackbird flew off into the next garden.

Joe awoke abruptly. He sat up in bed. It was starting to get light, but he knew it was too early to get up. Something had disturbed him. Was it just one of his dreams? He listened.

Suddenly he heard a high-pitched groaning, then some words shouted through the darkness.

He went to the door, and listened again. The sounds were coming from Dad's room. He crossed the landing, went into Ellen's room, and shook her by the shoulder.

'Ellen, wake up!'

'Mmmmm?' She stirred, then saw him. 'Joe? What is it?'

'It's Dad. Listen.'

There was a further burst of shouting, not so loud as before, but lasting longer. Ellen scrambled out of bed, and they hurried to Dad's room. Ellen hesitated, but there was no further sound. She pushed the door open.

Dad was sitting up in bed. By the light coming through the curtains, Joe saw his face—white and fearful, his eyes wide, his mouth open, his whole body shivering.

'They're trapped now, it's no good, they're trapped!' he whispered fiercely.

'Who is?' said Ellen, realizing he was having a nightmare.

Dad looked at her sharply. 'There was nothing else we could do, nurse,' he said.

Ellen looked at Joe. 'Go and wake up Aunty Muriel,' she told him. 'I'll stay here.'

14

She moved round to the side of the bed and, trying not to show how upset she was, took hold of Dad's hand.

'It's all right, Dad, it's only a dream,' she said. He was still shaking, and his hand was hot. His brown eyes, normally so gentle, looked wild and angry. He looked closely at Ellen, but didn't seem to recognize her. She felt even more upset: it was as if he was no longer with her, no longer Dad any more.

Then Aunty Muriel came in with Joe. She drew back the curtains, fetched a glass of water, found the thermometer, and took Dad's temperature. She looked worried.

'It's too early for the doctor,' she said, half to herself. 'Ellen, ring for an ambulance, quickly. Call 999, say your father has been taken ill, and tell them the address. Have you got that?'

'Yes. Is he very ill, Aunty?' Ellen asked, as she edged to the door.

'Just hurry and do what I say, child.'

Joe stood silently in the corner. He had never seen anyone really ill before. If Dad was going to hospital, it would be serious: did that mean he was going to die? What would happen then to him and Ellen, with Mum not here any more? He twisted the cord of his dressing-gown, feeling frightened.

Ellen came running back into the room. 'The man said they'll be here in a few minutes,' she said, and dropped down to her knees at the side of Dad's bed. She noticed his face was more relaxed now as he lay back on the pillow, and she felt his hand cooler.

Before long the ambulance arrived. Dad was lifted on to a stretcher and carried downstairs by two men in blue jerseys. As they reached the door, with the children right behind them, Dad raised up his hand. The men stopped. He turned his head and looked at Joe and Ellen.

'Dig for victory!' he shouted, with a strange smile.

Ellen saw the men look at each other, then move on out into the street. It was just getting light, and they could hear an early train rattling along in the distance. While Joe and Ellen stood helplessly on the doorstep, the men lifted Dad into the ambulance, closed the doors, and drove him away.

Chapter 2

THE HOME

Miss Snow, the welfare assistant, spoke briskly. 'Here we are, children. Quickly, out you get.'

Ellen and Joe climbed out of the car and stood on the pavement. They looked up at the notice hanging on the railings. 'Bethesda Children's Home' it said, in big brown letters. It reminds me of school, Ellen thought, as she gazed across a courtyard at a large grey building. But there's something different too. Then she noticed the windows on the ground floor had bars in them.

The two children picked up their suitcases and followed Miss Snow through the heavy iron gate. As they crossed the courtyard, Joe looked at the rows and rows of windows, and shuddered. How could a place like this be a home, he wondered?

Ellen still could not believe they had come to such a place. The events of the previous few days seemed like a dream, over which she had no control. Dad's illness meant that Aunty Muriel had stayed on for a while, and had tried desperately to get in touch with Mum. But a letter addressed to the hotel in Wales had been returned, marked 'Gone Away'.

Then she had tried to find someone else to look after them, but without success—they had no other close relations who might have been able to help. And then there had been the visits from men and women with briefcases and worried faces, and finally Aunty Muriel telling them they had been offered places in a Home the other side of London.

'It will only be for a short while,' she had said. 'Just long

17

enough to give us time to contact your mother, and sort things out.'

Ellen was so upset at what had happened to Dad, and the thought of having to stay with Aunty Muriel, that she hadn't understood what this other 'home' was. Even when Miss Snow had arrived in her car to take them there, neither Ellen nor Joe had really taken in what was happening. And now here they were, completely cut off from their family, as well as all their friends at school.

'Just wait here, and I'll see if Mr Turner is in his office,' Miss Snow said, as they reached the main door. She disappeared, leaving Joe and Ellen alone. In front of them stretched a long bare corridor. Joe caught the smell of cooking, and suddenly realized he was hungry.

'Will we have supper soon?' he asked Ellen.

'I expect so,' she replied.

'And will we have a room each, do you think?'

'I don't know, Joe,' she said, realizing how little she had thought about this cold, empty place. Secretly she hoped she and Joe would share a room; Joe was thinking the same.

Miss Snow joined them again. 'The superintendent is free now,' she said. 'This way. You can leave your cases here.' She led them down a side corridor, knocked on the brown door at the end and, without waiting for an answer, drew them into the room.

'These are the Duffy children, Mr Turner,' she said, speaking to a man standing with his back to them, looking out of the window. 'The Battersea lot, you remember?'

The man turned round, looked at them, and smiled slightly. 'Remembered!' he said briskly. He was quite old, with thin white hair falling across his forehead. 'Just in time for supper,' he continued, and sat down in the chair behind his desk. Ellen noticed that his eyes darted around the room, as though he, not they, were the strangers.

'Few words about Bethesda,' he said, poking a yellow pencil behind his ear. 'Good staff here. But no nonsense.

18

Play fair by them, they'll do the same.' He glanced at the ceiling. 'Aim is to take care of you. Home from home really. Takes a bit of getting used to. Any questions?'

Ellen looked at the pencil behind his ear. 'Do we have school here as well, or somewhere else?' she asked.

'Total service in Bethesda,' the man replied. 'Living and learning. Can't have one without the other. Next?'

Joe was uncertain. Was this odd man being friendly or not? He decided to risk it. 'Can you tell us where we sleep, please?' he said.

The man's eyes shifted to the wall, then back again. 'Gracious no,' he said. 'Snow's department. Get bogged down otherwise. Leave that to infantry.' He took the pencil from behind his ear, and began writing on a piece of paper.

Miss Snow came forward. 'That will do now: Mr Turner is a busy man. I'll show you to your rooms.' She bustled them out. As the door was closing Joe looked back, and saw Mr Turner drawing a circle in the air with his pencil.

They took up their suitcases, and followed Miss Snow along the corridor, up a flight of stairs, and along another long corridor. Ellen wondered where the other children were. There must be an awful lot of them in a building this size—perhaps even more than in their school? But so far they hadn't seen one other child.

Miss Snow stopped outside a red door, got out a big bunch of keys, and unlocked it. 'This is your dormitory,' she said to Ellen. She looked inside, and saw a small room with five beds on each side.

Ellen was shocked. 'Don't we have our own room?' she said, glancing anxiously at Joe, who was looking at the floor.

Miss Snow gave a small snort. 'Where do you think you are, luv, the Ritz?' she said. 'You all muck in together here you know. Now put your case on one of the unmade beds, young lady, and we'll go and find your brother's dormitory.'

'Aren't I in here as well?' Joe asked.

'Lord love-a-duck, what are you thinking of, young feller?' Miss Snow replied, chuckling to herself. 'No, the lads are over in the other block. This way.'

They followed her again, down more stairs, along other corridors. It seemed miles. Joe got more anxious with every step. All the corridors seemed the same, and why was there nobody around? Eventually Miss Snow stopped at another door, and unlocked it.

'A bit cosier this one,' Miss Snow said, looking around. Joe saw a small, dark, tiled room, with a high ceiling, and a bed in each corner. It had a strange smell, and felt very cold. He didn't think it was cosy at all.

'This will have to be yours, all the others are taken,' Miss Snow said. She took Joe's case from him, and put it on the bed nearest the window. 'Now we'll go to the dining-room. I dare say there'll still be some food left.'

More corridors, more stairs. They heard the low murmur of voices, getting nearer and nearer. Miss Snow stopped by a double door. As they went through, the sound increased suddenly and they stopped. They were in a large hall filled with children, sitting and eating at long tables that stretched down the hall.

'Just help yourselves, and find a place where you can,' Miss Snow said, and disappeared. Joe and Ellen stood uncertainly between the rows of tables. Then Ellen saw three women standing behind large silver containers at the far end of the hall.

'There's the food, Joe,' she said. As they walked between the tables, several children looked round. A few laughed and pointed, or nudged the person next to them; others just stared, then turned back to their food. Joe felt frightened. Who were all these children? How would he ever get to know them?

They reached the food table. 'Get yourselves a plate,' said one of the women. They did so, and the women ladled the food on to them. Ellen looked at the boiled potatoes and cabbage and the one tiny sausage, and made a face.

'Beggars can't be choosers,' another of the women said. 'You're lucky to get that, my girl, what with all this rationing and that still going on.' Ellen passed on, remembering the rations they had to live on during the war, and how Mum had still managed to make delicious meals.

They found two free places at the end of one table. The two boys next to Joe carried on talking in whispers, ignoring them. The girl on Ellen's right pushed her plate away, and looked at Ellen.

'New ginks, are yer?' she said.

'Yes,' replied Ellen.

'Where yer from, then?'

'Battersea.'

'Blimey, you've come a long way.'

'We're not staying very long. Just until our Dad's better.'

The girl smiled. Ellen noticed one of her front teeth was missing. 'That's what all the new ginks say.'

'What do you mean?'

'You'll see.' She looked across at Joe. 'Is 'e your brother, then?'

'Yes.' She was still thinking about what the girl had said. 'How long have you been here?'

'Since me Mum copped it in the bombing. Our 'ouse in Shoreditch got 'it by a rocket,' the girl replied, not seeming at all sad about it. Ellen remembered how lucky they had been to escape all that in Wales. Wales!—that was where Mum was now—or was she?

'Where's yer Mum, then?' the girl said, as if reading Ellen's mind.

'Oh, she's dead too,' she replied quickly, then blushed at what she had said. She looked at Joe, who was staring at her in surprise. 'At least, she's missing,' Ellen said hastily. She felt confused about Mum.

Just then the whistle blew. The children stopped talking. A woman stood up in the middle of the hall, and waited until there was silence.

21

'Supper duty tonight: Wilkins, Pearce, Castle and Allen,' she said. 'And I want a much better job done than last night. There were still crumbs under some of the chairs. Hands up last night's team. Right, you'll be on again tomorrow. And the next day and the next, until you get it right. Understood?'

'Yes, Miss Baxter,' came the reply from different parts of the hall.

'All right. Now lead out quietly, one table at a time— and don't let me catch any of you running in the corridors.'

Suddenly Joe began to panic. 'How do we get back to our bedrooms?' he whispered to Ellen.

'Don't you know yer room number?' the girl next to Ellen said.

'No,' Joe replied miserably. 'I forgot to look.'

'It's all right, I can remember them,' Ellen said. 'You were seventeen, and I was three. But I'm not sure how we get there.' She turned to the girl. 'Could you tell us?'

'I should coco, I'm in room three myself,' the girl replied. 'Come on.'

'Oh good. But my brother—'

'It's on the way, I'll show yer.'

After another long walk, they reached Joe's dormitory. The door was open. As they stood outside, Joe saw a group of boys at one end, chatting and giggling to themselves over something one of them was holding. He looked back at Ellen, fearful to be on his own.

She smiled at him, and squeezed his hand. 'You'll be all right, Joe. I'll come and collect you before breakfast.'

Joe watched his sister and the other girl move away. Then he walked into the dormitory, aware of the other boys watching him. He found his bed, and started unpacking, hoping they wouldn't notice his tears.

For the first few days Ellen and Joe had very little time to be homesick. Nearly every moment of the day seemed to be filled. In the mornings on weekdays there were lessons, when you were crammed into huge classrooms for arithmetic, English, geography and, once a week, nature study.

After lunch there was drill twice a week, and every day you had to do two hours' Useful Work, which meant doing some job around the place—cleaning the floors or windows, sweeping the leaves from the courtyard, helping the kitchen staff wash up lunch or get the evening meal ready.

Then between tea—a glass of milk and a biscuit—and supper you were expected to do your homework. Only in the evenings did you have a little bit of spare time. But what was there to do, apart from sit and talk, or read one of the battered comics or story books from the Home's small library?

There *was* one bright spot. Every evening, groups of children were let out to play in the grassy square at the back, which ran down to the railway line. During your half hour you could join in one of the games, or simply stand by the high wire fence at the edge of the railway track, and watch the trains steam by. But if it rained, you had to stay indoors with the other children.

Joe and Ellen, not knowing anyone else, spent as much of each day together as they could—which was not much, apart from mealtimes. They were in different classes for lessons, and never seemed to be in the same group for Useful Work. They weren't allowed into each other's dormitory, so most evenings there were only the games rooms, which were very noisy, or one of the two sitting-rooms, which were always full up anyway.

Ellen did make a couple of friends in her dormitory, including Annie, the girl she had sat next to on their first night. She soon found out what a useful person she was to know. She'd been in the Home for over a year, and knew exactly what each of the adults would let you get away with, which rules you had to obey and which you could get round.

'Baxter's the one yer 'ave to watch,' she said. The two of them were sitting on Ellen's bed on the second night after she and Joe had arrived. 'She likes ter make trouble, specially for us girls.'

'What happens if you break the rules?' Ellen asked anxiously.

'Depends 'oo catches yer,' Annie said, swinging her thin legs to and fro as she talked. 'Yer get black marks in the register, and they add 'em up at the end of the week. Every time yer get to ten, yer catch a walloping.'

'What, you mean the cane?'

'If yer lucky. Old Baxter uses a slipper, and that bleeding well hurts, I can tell yer.'

'Have you had that?'

'Nah, not for a year now. I keep out of trouble, see. 'S not worth it.'

For Joe life was more difficult. The other boys in his room seemed older than him—but maybe they were just taller and bigger? Although they told him what to do if he asked, most of the time they simply ignored him. He felt very left out.

It was the same in lessons. Everyone around him seemed to know lots of other children. Even the work didn't help. He found most of it much easier than at school. If you were quick at, say, arithmetic, like he was, you just had to wait until the slower ones caught up.

So he spent a lot of time in that first week looking out of the window. The desks and chairs in the classroom were on steps going up to the back, and from the back row Joe could see out on to the railway line. He liked especially to watch the trains travelling away from London, their steam flowing behind them as they pushed their way up the hill, and into the beginning of the countryside.

He remembered the last train journey he had made, when the whole family had come back from Wales last year. They had all been happy at that moment—Mum excited at the thought of getting back to London, Dad

24

happily smoking a cigarette, Ellen reading, and Joe with his nose to the window, taking in the scenery. Will it ever be like that again for us, he thought?

He still didn't understand what was going to happen to them. Supposing Dad didn't get better as quickly as they said he would? Where would they go then? Would they have to stay here until they were grown up? Most of all, why had Mum not been around to stop them being sent here?

Joe thought a lot about these questions during those first few days. On the Sunday, when a group of older children were taken on an outing, he and Ellen were at last able to be alone, and get a chance to talk. For once there was space in the sitting-rooms, and in one they found a window-seat free.

'How long do you think we'll have to stay here, Ellen?' Joe said.

'Not very long, I hope,' she replied.

'Do you hate it too?'

'Of course I do! Who *wouldn't* hate a place like this? But we just have to put up with it for a bit, Joe.'

'Until Dad's better?'

'Yes.'

'But why can't they say how long that will be?'

'Because the doctor's not sure, I suppose. But we'll know as soon as he is. Then Dad'll come and fetch us.'

But Ellen knew nothing was certain. She had a horrible feeling it might be a long time before Dad was well enough to return home, and take them away from here. It was so hard being without him and Mum; it meant that you had to decide everything for yourself, and she didn't like that. She knew she would have to look after Joe, and try and help him not to be too sad.

'Have you made any friends yet, Joe?' she asked.

'Not really; the other boys have friends already.'

'Don't worry, I'm sure you will.' There was silence between them.

25

'Ellen.'

'Yes, Joe?'

'Do you know why all these children are here?'

'I know about some of them—Annie's told me. Most of them lost their mums and dads in the war, and they don't have anywhere else to go. Some of them are waiting to be adopted.'

'What's adopted?'

'Annie says it's when you go to someone else's family when you haven't got your own any more. They look after you instead of your own parents.'

'Is that what might happen to us?'

'No, we've still got our mum and dad. It's just they're not at home at the moment. It's not the same.'

'Good. I don't want to be anyone else's child.'

'Nor do I, Joe.'

Lying in bed that night, Ellen thought about this conversation. She wondered if it was right what she had told Joe. Perhaps you *could* be adopted even if your mum and dad were alive? But then surely you couldn't have two families at once? That wouldn't be allowed. But supposing you were adopted, and it turned out your new mum and dad didn't love you. What happened then? Did you have to stay with them, or would they send you back to the Home?

The more she turned over these questions in her mind, the more confused she became. It was a long time before she was able to get to sleep.

Chapter 3
GETTING AWAY

At supper the next night Miss Baxter asked all the girls in room three to go to their dormitory straight after the meal. As they filed out of the hall, Ellen caught up with Annie.

'Why does she want to see just us?' she asked her friend.

'It's about Clare, if yer want to know what I think,' Annie replied.

'Why, what's she done?'

'Only done a bunk, 'asn't she.'

Ellen stopped in the middle of the corridor. 'Run away? When?'

'This morning, while they were on the outing. Eileen told me at supper: she was with 'er.'

'What happened?'

'They were walking over these fields, see, and all of a sudden Clare says to Eileen, "Don't say anything", and she hides behind a hedge. No one misses her for ages, and then they sends out a search party. Couldn't find her, though.'

'But where would she go. Aren't her mum and dad dead?'

'Yeah, but she's got an older brother. She told me about him, but I can't for the life of me remember where 'e lives.'

As they hurried on, Ellen thought about Clare. She had seemed a shy girl, frightened by everything going on around her. She hardly spoke to the other children. When she did, her voice was so quiet you had to lean towards her to catch what she said. Ellen couldn't imagine her having the courage to run away.

When the girls reached their dormitory they had a

surprise. There, sitting on her bed, was Clare. Dressed in a coat with a suitcase beside her, she sat with head lowered, her hands together. At the end of her bed stood Miss Baxter.

It was the first time Ellen had seen Miss Baxter close to. She could understand why the other children were frightened of her. Her face was small and pale, almost white, and her thin lips seemed to disappear into her mouth. As she stood there with arms folded, Ellen noticed her small eyes, green and cold, which seemed to get even smaller when she looked at you.

'I don't suppose you expected your friend back quite so soon, did you?' She looked at each of them in turn. Her voice was shrill and unpleasant. 'This girl's stupid action has taken up a lot of staff time. I will not have any more of this nonsense. You don't know how lucky you all are being here. It may not be your home, but it's better than the gutter, isn't it? That's where you would be otherwise.'

She looked at Clare, and sniggered. 'As for you, girl, we'll have no more nonsense before your journey. As you clearly don't want to be with your friends, we'll find you a room of your own. You'll have lots of time there to think about your misguided adventure.'

She turned back to the group. 'I imagine you all understand how serious this matter is?'

'Yes, Miss Baxter,' came the chorus.

'If I catch a single one of you trying anything like this . . .' She let the threat hang in the air, and moved to the door. 'Come on, Bates, what are you waiting for?'

Clare got off the bed, and walked across the room. As she passed Ellen she looked up, and Ellen thought she smiled slightly. Then she was swept away by Miss Baxter.

Ellen was puzzled. She went and sat with Annie on her bed. 'Why do you think Clare ran away?' she asked her.

'That's easy-peasy: she didn't fancy going to Australia.'

'Australia! Why would she go there?'

'She'd been chosen for the next group, that's why. Then

she changed 'er mind, but old Baxter said it was too late. Said they'd already got 'er tickets, and fixed up this 'ome for 'er.'

'You mean children get sent to Australia from here?'

'Yeah: or it might be Canada or South Africa, for some of 'em.'

'But what for?'

'So's you can start a new life out there, that's what they say.'

'Would you go, Annie?'

'Dunno, I might do. This place is a dump anyway. Sometimes I think, anything to get away.'

'Why haven't you, then?'

''aven't felt like it.'

Ellen shifted her position. 'What will happen to Clare now?' she said.

'She'll get isolation for a week.'

'What's that?'

'She'll be in a room by 'erself, and she'll 'ave 'er meals taken in, and 'ave to do lots of 'omework instead of lessons.'

'That's horrible!' Ellen exclaimed. 'She'll get so lonely!'

'It's Baxter's favourite punishment.'

'Is she allowed any visitors?'

'No.'

'Well, I shall go and see her anyway! I don't care about mean old Baxter. Where is the isolation room?'

Ellen was upset. She hardly knew Clare, but she felt sorry for her, and angry that a girl like her should be treated like this. She decided to visit her as soon as possible. Annie tried to stop her, saying she would get into trouble. But Ellen didn't mind about that: it was worth it.

The next morning, between breakfast and lessons, Annie pointed out the isolation room to Ellen, and then kept watch for her at one end of the corridor. Ellen knocked at the door. No answer. She knocked again. Still no reply. She looked towards Annie, and saw her giving the signal that

29

someone was coming. Quickly she turned the handle, and edged into the room.

Clare was sitting at a desk by the window, looking out. She turned round, and her eyes opened wide.

'Ellen!' she said, in her soft voice. 'What are you doing here?'

'I thought you might like a visitor.'

'You could get into awful trouble, you know.'

'Too bad,' Ellen said, looking round the bare room. 'What's it like in here?'

'It's all right. At least I can see the hill.'

Ellen came to the window. Beyond the railway track a hill rose up gently, dotted with large trees, their leaves already brown. She was reminded of Battersea Park, and of Dad, working on the flower-bed under the giant oak tree on the riverside.

She turned back to Clare. 'How did they catch you?' she asked.

Clare sighed. 'A policeman stopped me in the next village. They'd been told to look out for me.'

'But where were you going?'

'I was trying to get to my brother's house—it wasn't very far.'

Ellen moved to Clare's bed, and sat down. 'And do you have to go to Australia after all?' she asked her.

'I think so,' Clare replied, looking sad.

Ellen was puzzled. 'But if you don't want to . . .?'

'I did at first. They read out a letter from a boy and a girl who went there last year. It sounded exciting. I thought I'd like it more than being here. But then I got scared: it seemed such a long way away.'

'But they can't *make* you go, can they?'

'Miss Baxter says it's all arranged, it's too late to change my mind.'

Ellen wondered if this was true. But even if it wasn't, what could Clare do about it?

Clare came and sat on the bed. 'Maybe I'll like it there?'

she said. 'You can work on a farm some of the time.'
Suddenly she became anxious. 'Ellen, you better go.
Someone will be bringing my school work any minute
now.'

'All right,' Ellen said, getting up. 'But I'll come and see
you again soon.'

'Are you sure you should?' Clare said, frowning.

'Of course.' Ellen paused at the door. 'Is there anything
you want me to bring you?'

'No thanks, I'm all right,' Clare replied.

'Bye then.'

'Bye. And thanks for coming.'

Ellen slipped out of the room. As she closed the door,
Mr Turner came round the corner. Ellen hesitated. Had he
seen her leave Clare's room? As they came near each other,
Ellen held her breath. Mr Turner frowned, nodded,
glanced at the ceiling, and moved on. Ellen hurriedly went
to collect her books for the first lesson.

'And I want to see Ellen Duffy in Mr Turner's office after
this meal.'

The children sitting near her at the table glanced at Ellen,
who blushed. Joe, sitting opposite, looked worried.

'What's that for, Ellen?' he asked.

'I don't know,' she replied. 'Perhaps it's news about
Dad?'

'But then she'd say my name as well, wouldn't she?'

'Yes, I suppose she would.'

Ellen knew what she was wanted for. When she got to
Mr Turner's office, Miss Baxter was sitting in his chair.
Ellen thought she looked paler than ever.

'I've called you here, Duffy, because I'm told you've
been breaking the rules,' she began. 'You were seen coming
out of Clare Bates's room. You know that is strictly
forbidden. Well?'

Ellen gripped the arm of the chair. 'I don't think it's right

31

for someone to be on their own like that,' she said, wishing her voice wouldn't shake.

Miss Baxter's cold eyes looked at her. 'I see. And since when have you been making the rules here, young lady?'

'But it's not fair—'

'Silence! How dare you argue?' Ellen saw her piercing green eyes open wide. 'Clare Bates is taking her punishment; you will do the same. You will not be allowed to play for two weeks. You will help the cleaning staff for an hour every morning before breakfast. If I catch you again, the punishment will be more severe. Now leave.'

Ellen walked down the corridor, aware that her heart was beating fast. She hated Miss Baxter—she'd never hated anybody more fiercely! Nothing was going to stop her going to visit Clare again, even if it did mean a beating.

Later she told Joe what had happened. They were sitting on a bench under one of the barred windows in the courtyard. A group of children near them played with an old tennis ball, throwing it to one another.

Joe listened. He hoped he wouldn't ever have to face Miss Baxter. He was glad Ellen had said what she thought, but he knew he couldn't have done that. He also knew he wouldn't have broken the rules in the first place.

'Are you really going to visit Clare again?' he asked Ellen, anxiously.

'Yes. She's really miserable about going to Australia.'

Every day since they came to Bethesda, Joe and Ellen had been hoping to hear news about Dad. But when it finally came, it was bad news.

Ellen sat in her room and read the letter from Aunty Muriel. Although Dad was now out of hospital, the doctor had advised several months' rest. He had been moved to a nursing home near Eastbourne, where he would be well looked after. There was no news of Mum—except a postcard from North Wales which said she was all right, and that there was no need to worry about her. Then Ellen read the last part of the letter:

'Your Home has written asking whether Uncle Tom and I would consider having the two of you. You know I'd like to help, but unfortunately we don't have any spare rooms. But maybe another family could be found who would be prepared to foster you? I do think that would be good for you both.

'Meanwhile, I have accepted, on behalf of your father, the Home's generous offer to try and place you somewhere for a while. Naturally, your Uncle Tom and I hope that before too long your father will be able to resume a normal life, and the family be reunited.'

Ellen was shattered. She realized how badly she had missed Dad. Now it seemed she and Joe would have to stay in the Home for several more months, possibly a year. How could they stand that, she thought, her eyes filling with tears.

Later, when she had time to recover from the first shock, she found Joe in the courtyard. As they walked alongside the railings, she gently told him the news.

'But I don't want to be a foster,' he said immediately.

'Nor do I, Joe. But if we don't agree, we might have to stay here a year or more.'

Joe felt upset and confused. He hated being at Bethesda. Every day he longed for their time here to end. Often he thought back to Wales, to the freedom he and Ellen had there, to the expeditions and adventures, the times they had walked and played in the valleys, and swum in the cold, clear lakes. Here, in the dreariness of the Home, he felt as if someone had shut him in a darkened room and thrown away the key.

Yet the idea of living in someone else's home seemed just as bad. I don't want any pretend parents, he said to himself, I want my own Mum and Dad.

Ellen decided she would pay another visit to Clare in the morning. But at breakfast she discovered she was too late. For once, the bell for announcements rang before the meal, rather than after it. Miss Baxter rose, her face hard and angry.

'I have a very important announcement,' she began. 'We have reason to believe that Clare Bates and John Aitkenhead have run away.'

There were a few gasps, and some whispering around the hall. Miss Baxter's voice rose. 'Silence! This is a very serious matter indeed. The police have been informed, of course. Those two children are our responsibility—as all of you are. Now, if any of you have the slightest idea where these two children have gone, it's your duty to let us know. If we find someone has tried to keep this information from us, they will be punished severely.'

She looked fiercely at the rows of faces. No one stirred or spoke. Ellen made sure she didn't catch Miss Baxter's eye. She smiled to herself: she guessed Clare would be well on her way to her brother's house by now. She imagined the two runaways sitting cheerfully, in one of those green country coaches, knowing every minute took them further away from the Home.

Miss Baxter was angrier than ever. 'All right, if nobody will come forward here, maybe they will on their own,' she said. 'I'd like anyone who knows anything to come to Mr Turner's office straight after breakfast. That is all.'

Ellen looked across at Joe, and caught his eye. They exchanged secret smiles. Ellen was so pleased for Clare—that would teach them to try and force her to go to Australia. But she was also sorry to have lost a new friend. I don't suppose I'll see her or ever hear from her again, she thought sadly.

But she was wrong. Two days later there was an envelope in the post for her. Ellen found a plain white card inside. There was no address or date on it, simply a few words in blue ink: 'Just to let you know we made it! Thanks for

34

being kind and visiting me. Clare.' This message made Ellen happy for the first time since they had been in the Home.

She told Joe the news, and for the rest of the morning found herself smiling every now and then, at the thought of Clare's escape.

But at lunch time she had a shock. Miss Baxter announced that she wanted to see her in her office, but this time with Joe. When they arrived, they discovered Mr Turner there too, sitting behind his desk, with Miss Baxter standing sternly alongside.

'Bad business, this,' Mr Turner began, his eyes darting all over the place, but never looking at Joe or Ellen. 'Frowned upon, you know.' He stopped, and looked uncertainly at Miss Baxter, who moved closer to Ellen, and held up an envelope in front of her face.

'So, you *did* know about Bates's plan,' Miss Baxter said, menacingly.

'Where did you get that from?' Ellen burst out angrily, realizing one of the staff must have taken it from the cupboard by her bed. 'That's my property, it's private.'

'That's how you'd like to keep it, I'm sure,' Miss Baxter said. 'Fortunately we recognized the handwriting on the envelope. Now, where has she gone? Out with it! It's quite clear she discussed her plans with you.'

Ellen suddenly realized she was no longer frightened of Miss Baxter. 'What if she did: that's not against the law, is it?' she asked boldly.

Miss Baxter's mouth became thinner than ever. She looked across to Mr Turner, who coughed nervously, passed her a file, and started chewing his yellow pencil.

Miss Baxter glanced through the file. 'We've had a lot of trouble from you already, Duffy,' she said, looking up again at Ellen. 'I'm beginning to think Bethesda isn't quite the right place for you and your brother.'

Joe and Ellen looked at each other, wondering what Miss Baxter meant. Was there a chance of moving?

'I imagine you know that Bates and Aitkenhead were

due to go to Australia shortly?' Miss Baxter continued. 'All the arrangements had been made—their tickets paid for, their accommodation settled. Now, suddenly, we are two children short in the group. We can't afford such a situation.'

Joe was suddenly afraid. Did she mean they were going to send Ellen and him to Australia? He turned to see what Ellen was thinking, and saw her cheeks reddening.

'You can't *make* us go there!' she said fiercely.

Miss Baxter smiled grimly. 'We only want to do what is in the best interests of our children. Fortunately, your aunt has passed on to us the responsibility of finding you a new home. Of course, we do sometimes place children in foster homes over here—*if* they're helpful and co-operative. But in many cases, a new start in a new country is the better solution.'

She snapped the file shut. 'We have to decide by tomorrow which two children to add to the Australian group. You two are at the top of our list, isn't that so, Mr Turner?'

'Exactly so,' he replied, looking for something in the drawer of his desk. 'Absolute priority.'

'Well, Duffy, would you like to help us and help yourself at the same time?'

Ellen looked anxiously at Joe. 'I'll have to talk with my brother,' she said. 'Come on, Joe.'

For the rest of the day, the two of them could think about nothing else but the idea of going to Australia.

Joe realized all he knew about the country was that it was hot, and had lots of kangaroos hopping about. He was not even sure where it was on the map: did you go by train or boat? It seemed very frightening to be going off somewhere completely new. But as he thought more, he wondered whether it would be any worse than staying at Bethesda, packed together day and night with so many other children, with the grown-ups seeming to be against you all the time?

Ellen was half excited, half fearful of the idea. At school she had been interested in geography, and often wondered what places like Alice Springs and the Great Barrier Reef and Tasmania were really like. It might be exciting to find out. Clare had said it was only for a year, and by then Dad would be well again.

But she was worried on Joe's behalf—he seemed so young to go far away to a strange new land. She also thought about Dad. Could they bear to leave him when he was so unwell? Wouldn't they miss him dreadfully? And what about Mum . . . why wouldn't she tell them where she was? She also hated the idea of betraying Clare, especially after she had tried so hard to get away. She knew she herself would cope better than Clare would in a different country.

In the early evening she and Joe met up in the courtyard, and walked along by the railings.

'What will be best?' Joe asked. 'I can't make up my mind.'

They walked slowly, Joe dragging a piece of wood along the railings. Ellen stopped. 'I've thought all day about it, Joe,' she said. 'I don't want to tell them where Clare is. But if you really hate the idea of going, then I will.'

Joe threw his stick high across the courtyard. 'I don't mind going if we have to,' he said.

Joe looked around the crowded dockside. He had never seen so many children together. Everywhere he looked there were groups of boys and girls talking excitedly, laughing, jostling each other, or pointing up at the huge ship that loomed above them.

He noticed some of the children were younger than him. A few of the smaller girls were clutching dolls. Others were sitting quietly on their suitcases, looking sad. He saw one girl crying, and being comforted by an older girl.

A voice boomed out close to him. 'Bethesda children next for boarding.' A red-faced man with a sheet of paper was waving them into a line.

Joe picked up his small suitcases. Ellen smiled down at him. 'Not long now, Joe,' she said.

'All right, in twos, follow me,' the man called out. The group moved towards the gangplank. As they walked up it, Ellen looked back down at the dockside. At the back, separated by a rope from the children, she saw some grown-ups waving—mothers and fathers, she supposed. A flicker of fear ran through her. She realized again what a big step they were taking, and how little she and Joe knew about what lay ahead.

Once on board they were allowed to put their suitcases into a cabin, and go back on deck to watch the ship leave. As it inched away from the dock, Ellen looked across to the city, and saw the familiar sight of bombed buildings. Beyond she saw the green of the countryside, reminding her of the carefree months they had spent in Wales.

As the ship began to increase speed, she saw a few figures walking along the part of the dockside that curved round the harbour, and waving to the ship. One by one they dropped off, until there was only one woman left, dressed in a black coat, and now breaking into a gentle run. Then she came to the end of the dock, and the ship turned away from the land. As the waving figure became smaller and smaller, Ellen wondered how long it would be before she saw Mum and Dad again.

Chapter 4

THE VOYAGE

The first few hours on board were full of excitement. Although the boys and girls slept in separate quarters on the lower deck, Joe and Ellen were across the corridor from each other. This seemed like a good start.

Once they had unpacked, they were taken to the large dining-room in the middle of the ship, to have tea. It was very different from tea at the Home. Here there were sandwiches and cakes and orange squash, and music coming over the loudspeaker, and you could eat as much as you felt like, and talk as loudly as you wanted.

The captain came in. A small cheerful man, he welcomed them aboard ship, told them it would be their home for the next six weeks, and that he was sure they would all be very good sailors by the time they reached Australia. He took out a large plan of the ship, pinned it up on the wall, and showed them which parts they were allowed to explore, and which were just for the crew. Then he said '*Bon voyage*', gave the children a salute, and left.

After that, a woman called Miss Reed got up and told them about the activities they could take part in during their journey, what time the meals were, and when they had to be in bed. 'And now you are free to explore the ship. But please, children, remember what the captain said about where you can go. And don't forget your bedtimes.'

'Just imagine, Joe,' Ellen said, as they made their way with other children to the top deck, 'all that free time! I can hardly believe it.'

'We don't have to do any cleaning, do we?' Joe said anxiously, still not quite sure of their luck.

'I'm sure we don't,' Ellen replied. 'They would have told us by now.' She did a little skip along the corridor.

They reached the top deck. It was already dark as they moved out to the thick wooden rail near the front of the ship. 'Look at all those lights!' Joe said, pointing across the water. Ellen saw a glistening row of lights in the middle distance, cutting the sea and sky in half. Some of them seemed to be winking at them, saying *Bon voyage*.

'Where is that place?' Joe asked wonderingly.

'Some town or other,' Ellen said vaguely, caught up by the magic of the scene.

'Yes, but which one? Is it still England?'

'I expect it's France,' Ellen replied, remembering her geography lessons. She turned away from the lights, and looked at the sea ahead. The moon had the sky to itself, and in its light she watched the stillness of the water as the ship drew them steadily towards their new, unknown home.

Joe found that first night on board difficult. Twenty boys were crammed into one cabin, and there was even less room here than in the Home. Most of the boys were on bunk beds, but two were on mattresses on the floor, and Joe and one other were in hammocks. At first he liked the idea—this is what real sailors do, he thought. His hammock hung between two wooden posts, and as he lay on it he could feel the pulse of the engine, and the slight movement of the ship.

But soon he began to feel less comfortable, as the hammock began to dig in to his back. He tried turning on his side, and immediately tipped himself on to the floor. It took some time to get the hammock steady enough to get back in, but soon he felt uncomfortable again. He was on the point of falling asleep when a boy cried out loudly. Joe was so startled he fell out again. Now exhausted, he gathered up his sheet and blanket and pillow, lay down on the floor, and fell into a deep sleep.

In the girls' room, Ellen was pleased to get one of the top bunk beds. She lay listening to the breathing of the other girls, and thinking back over the day—the feeling of relief she had as they left the Home, the thrill of seeing fields and trees again as the train sped through the countryside, and then her sudden fear as the ship pulled away from England.

She slipped into sleep—but then awoke with a start, trembling with fear. For a moment she couldn't think where she was. Then she remembered. But why have I woken so suddenly, she thought? What was it that scared me? Then she realized she had been dreaming.

Unable to sleep, she started to piece together her dream. She remembered approaching a high wall, climbing up a ladder set against it, and sitting astride the wall. On the other side, just a few feet away, a train was moving past very slowly. She could see into the carriages. But who was in them? Oh yes, in one she saw herself and Joe, and in another Clare. But the strange thing was, Mum was also there, sitting on top of a carriage, smoking a cigarette with one hand, with the other shading her eyes and looking back along the track.

Ellen remembered there had been something odd about the driver—ah yes, he wore a large green cloak, and instead of filling the boiler with coal, he was staring at Ellen as she sat on the wall, and looking—no, it wasn't a man, it was Miss Baxter, she remembered that now. Then she suddenly realized the train was about to cross a bridge over the river, but the bridge had a large gap in it. Ellen screamed to Mum to jump, but she didn't hear her, even though Ellen screamed and screamed . . . and then woke up.

Ellen shivered. She wished these nightmares would stop: she'd never had one until she and Joe went to Bethesda. At the Home she had had two or three a week, though she hadn't liked to say anything to Joe about it. Always when she woke she felt terrified for a moment, before realizing where she was; and tonight it was the same. She drew the blanket around her neck, and lay there, watching the light gradually grow whiter and sharper round the edges of the cabin window.

For the first few days the weather was glorious, and the children spent most of the time on deck. Of the two adults with the Bethesda group, Mr Morris and Miss Reed, Miss Reed stayed in her cabin most of the time; but Mr Morris organized games and races and quizzes to keep them occupied.

Ellen joined in many of these, and got to know some of the other children. At other times she liked to lean on the rail at the stern of the ship, and watch the trail of foam stretching out into the distance behind them, as the gulls circled and screeched overhead. At these moments, looking back towards England and home, she always thought of Dad. She would remember the strange, awful expression on his face the morning he went into hospital, and wonder if he would be the same Dad she knew from before his illness.

Joe thought less about home than Ellen did. He was usually too busy. He was annoyed that it wasn't possible to play football on the ship, but he happily took part in the races, and in many of the indoor games. One of the other boys had brought a chess set along, and Joe learned to play. He also had his copy of *Treasure Island* that Mum had given him for his last birthday. When he tired of the games he would find a shady spot on deck, and lose himself in his favourite adventure.

After a week, the weather suddenly changed. When Joe and Ellen came out on deck one morning, they saw a huge slab of black cloud spreading itself down the side of the sky. The wind came at them strongly from a different direction. Ellen noticed the gulls were no longer following them. Soon a few spots of rain brushed their cheeks, and as they turned to go back down the iron stairway, it began to come down heavily.

42

'No races today,' Joe said, as they got under cover, and gazed through the window on to the already soaking deck. 'Just when I wanted to beat Michael Wright.'

'I wonder where the seagulls go when it rains?' Ellen said. 'Do you think they try and find land?'

'I don't know,' Joe replied, wondering how soon the deck would be dry enough for his race.

But it was quite a while before Joe was able to go out on deck. For the rest of that day the rain fell continuously. Sometimes the sea itself became invisible to the children gazing through the windows. Later the sky darkened further, the wind increased, and a tremendous storm began.

As the thunder cracked over their heads, the children grew excited. Even the rolling of the ship seemed great fun to Ellen and Joe. With some of the other children, they played at trying to walk in a straight line along the corridors, or pretending to be drunk as the ship rose and fell.

But before long Ellen began to feel ill, and left Joe to go back to the cabin. There she found several other girls sitting or lying on the bunks or mattresses, groaning, or just looking pale and unhappy. One girl jumped up from her bed and ran past Ellen, clutching her stomach. She returned soon after, walking slowly to her bed. 'I feel as if I'm going to die,' she said, turning her face to the wall.

Ellen slept little that night. Other girls kept getting up to go to the bathroom. One girl began to cry. Although the girl in the bunk above her tried to comfort her, the quiet sobs continued, stopping now and then as the rolls of thunder broke over the ship.

Ellen was unable to be sick, though she badly wanted to be. Sometimes the feeling went away, and then her mind turned towards the end of their journey. She realized how little she knew about what lay ahead. Although she knew

43

she and Joe were to go to something called a farm school, she had no idea where it was—she couldn't even remember its name. It had all happened so quickly, and she had been so busy thinking about leaving Dad, and wondering if Aunty Muriel would be able to get in touch with Mum, that the details had not seemed important.

But now all kinds of questions knocked at her mind's door. What kind of farm was it? Which animals would they be working with? Would there be other English children there, or would they all be Australian?

She had only met one person from Australia, and she had been a bit peculiar: a woman in a café in Wales, who wore a large floppy hat, and talked so loudly that all the Welsh people stopped to listen. Were they all like that, she wondered? She remembered the woman came from Sydney, and wondered if she and Joe would be able to go there.

The memory of Wales turned her thoughts again to Mum. Although she missed her terribly, she also half understood why she had gone away. Mum often seemed to be somewhere else. Ellen used to come into the kitchen and find her leaning on her elbow in a dream, the meal preparations quite forgotten. At other times, when the two of them had gone for walks through the Welsh countryside, talking in the way that Ellen loved, Mum would stop suddenly and gaze into the distance, as if their conversation had never happened.

Just then the ship gave a particularly heavy roll, and Ellen was pulled back into the present, where she stayed, uncomfortably, for the rest of the night.

Breakfast next morning was very different from the day before. There were only a few grown-ups there, and very few of the children. Those that did come didn't have much of an appetite. Joe seemed to be one of the few unaffected by the ship's movements. Ellen found him eating away happily, and talking to his new friend Michael.

'Good storm, wasn't it?' he said, as Ellen joined them.

44

'How can you *say* that, Joe?' she replied, still not sure if she wanted any breakfast.

'Because we were allowed to stay up late,' Joe replied, looking across at Michael.

His friend grinned. 'Yeah, and we played pirates in the corridor for hours,' he said. 'Mr Morris was too ill to tell us off.'

Ellen watched him attack his bowl of cereal. 'Where-abouts are you going in Australia?' she asked.

'Me?' he said, looking up. 'Dunno—don't care.' Ellen noticed the fierce expression. She hoped he wouldn't get Joe into trouble.

'Maybe you'll come to our farm school?' Joe said.

'Nah, I don't want to be a rotten farmer. I'm going to be a pilot and fly a Spitfire.' And he circled his piece of bread round his head, making a loud, whining sound.

'Do they have Spitfires in Australia?' Joe asked.

''Course they do, stupid.' He swallowed the last of his bread. 'Come on, I'll race you to the cabin.'

Joe glanced at Ellen. 'All right,' he said. He scrambled out of his seat and followed Michael.

Although the storm ended that morning, the bad weather continued. The rain clattered on the deck and streamed down the side of the white lifeboats, while the wind blew fiercely off the sea. After that first burst of sun and freedom, the children found it hard to stay inside.

Some grown-ups suffered from sickness worse than the children, and were forced to stay in their cabins most of the time, as the high winds battered the ship. So many of the games and activities didn't happen. The children became more and more bored and restless. The ship's crew were kindly and did what they could to help, but they had little time to spare.

One morning at breakfast, Mr Morris announced that the rain had stopped, and the children would be able to go on deck once again. 'But a word of warning,' he said. 'The wind's still very strong, so you must keep to the lower deck, and not go anywhere you shouldn't.'

Ellen still felt unwell, but Joe could hardly wait to get out. He and Michael were first on deck, and were soon joining in the handball games, the deck quoits and the relay races. Joe felt the wind and spray on his cheeks, and all the dreariness of the last few days was quite forgotten.

After another couple of hours of games after lunch, most of the children had had enough. Warm and happy, they ambled inside, leaving Joe, Michael and two other boys.

'Let's explore,' Michael said, and marched off along the deck, followed by Joe and the others. They walked to the stern, holding on to the rail. The ship dipped heavily as it cut through the waves. Joe saw that the gulls were back overhead, in greater numbers than before.

The end part of the stern was separated from the rest by a chain, on which there hung a notice: 'No Passengers Beyond This Point'. Joe could see why it was there. Each time the ship dropped into a valley between the waves, a lot of water poured through the back of the ship, smashed against the side nearest to them, and then ran back under the railings.

The boys watched, fascinated. Then Michael turned to Joe, his eyes sparkling. 'Let's beat the waves!' he said.

'What do you mean?' Joe asked anxiously.

'While the water's going back, you have to see how near the back of the ship you can get before the next wave comes.'

'But we're not allowed through there,' one of the other boys said, pointing to the sign.

'Who cares about a stupid notice!' Michael shouted. In a second he was under the chain. He hesitated, then dashed a few yards forward, stopped, waited at the ready looking back over his shoulder, and as the next wave broke through the railings, dashed back to the group.

'That wasn't very far!' said one of the other boys scornfully.

Michael frowned. 'That was just a practice,' he said. 'Watch this!'

Joe wanted to tell him to stop, but thought it might seem a bit cowardly. This time Michael went much further, and turned ready to sprint back. Then Joe heard a voice from behind and above, calling: 'Hey, come away from there, you young idiot!' He saw Michael glance back in their direction. Joe looked round to where the voice had come from. He saw one of the crew beckoning frantically to Michael. Joe looked back to the stern, and saw Michael fixed to the deck, gaping up at the man. At that moment another wave broke through the railings.

'Michael! Run!' Joe shouted. He saw his friend look behind him, start to run, slip, pick himself up, and then disappear under a huge wave, which lifted him and smashed him against the rail.

Joe looked at the other boys, and they at him. None of them could move. Suddenly two sailors rushed past them, leaping the chain as they went. As the wave disappeared Joe saw Michael lying underneath the railing. He was quite still. The two men knelt over him. Then one gathered him quickly in his arms, and brought him back out of reach of the next wave.

As they passed Joe, the sailor walking behind said, 'Come away now, lads, quickly.'

'Will he be all right?' Joe asked, his stomach tight with fear.

'Pray to God he is!' the man said grimly, as they followed the sailor carrying Michael.

Joe had never for an instant thought about God before. Now he whispered under his breath, 'Please let Michael live, God, *please* let him live.'

The water was still, at last. As Ellen stood near the rail, she felt for the first time how huge and unending the sea was.

At the same time she realized how small the ship was, as it moved quietly through the calm, silver-blue water.

She looked back on deck, where the other children waited silently. She had never been to a funeral before. She wasn't sure what you had to do. She knew Michael was to be buried at sea; Mr Morris had told them that. But she hadn't liked to ask what that meant. She hoped it didn't mean his body would just be thrown straight into the sea.

She glanced across at Joe. He was standing in front of one of the lifeboats, with the other two boys who had been with him that afternoon. Ellen had made sure she stayed with Joe as much as possible over the last three days. With the others Joe had tried to be brave, but once alone with her he gave in to his tears. Ellen tried to think what Mum would have done if she were here. She remembered the stories she used to tell them at bedtime. So when Joe was calmer, she re-told those she could remember, holding Joe's hand while he sat, white and exhausted.

A thin, high whistle broke into Ellen's thoughts. She saw four men coming through the rows of children, carrying a box on their shoulders. As they passed Ellen, she tried to imagine Michael's body inside, but found she couldn't do so: all she could think of was his playing Spitfires with his bread. She noticed the serious expressions on the faces of the sailors, and wondered if the box was heavy. She saw it was made from different kinds of wood, and in the corner she noticed, printed in red, the words 'Fragile: This Way Up'.

The men arrived at the table where the captain and Mr Morris stood. They placed the box on a board on the table, and placed a sheet over it. The captain removed his cap. The other sailors did the same. The whistling noise stopped. Then Mr Morris made a short speech about Michael. Ellen couldn't hear all the words, but she understood that Michael's parents had been killed in the war, and that he was going to Australia to 'start a new life'.

When Mr Morris had finished, the whistling began again.

The sailors lifted the board and carried the box slowly to the rail. They rested the board on it, and then at a signal from the captain, they let the box slide off from under the sheet and disappear overboard. Ellen listened for the splash, but could hear nothing. She wondered if the box would float, but decided it was probably too heavy.

The men turned back to face everyone else, and saluted. After that the grown-ups sang a hymn. It was a lovely one that Ellen hadn't heard before. It made her feel sad for the first time that day.

When the music ended the sailors put their caps on. Ellen found Joe, and they walked silently back along the deck.

For once, Joe wasn't looking forward to Christmas. Even though three weeks had passed since Michael's death, he was still unable to think of much else.

It was especially hard first thing in the morning. Sometimes when he woke up, he would forget for a moment what had happened. Then everything would come back. He found it so hard not to think of Michael's body, lying at the bottom of the sea. He would go over those terrible few seconds again and again, as if by doing so he could change what had happened, and bring Michael back to life. What if I had told him to stop after that first time, he kept asking himself? I know Ellen says it wouldn't have made any difference, he would have just gone anyway; but how does she know for sure?

He looked around the ship's dining-room, now being made ready for the Christmas party. Under the Christmas tree, the adults had put lots of small presents—one for each child, Mr Morris had explained. Joe felt he didn't deserve one. And what would Michael have had if he'd still been alive?

'Pass that streamer up, Joe,' Ellen said, from the top of the step ladder.

Joe handed her another row of coloured paper, and she fixed it to the wall. Michael's death had shocked Ellen, too. But she at least had something else to think about: getting Joe back into normal life. The trouble was, nothing seemed normal any more. Nobody said much about Michael's death, but you could see all the children were thinking about it. Nobody ran or laughed, or wanted to play games. They had been forbidden to go out on deck except with an adult—but no one wanted to go anyway now. There seemed nothing to do but sit and wait.

As she fixed the decorations, Ellen thought of Christmas Eve the previous year. She remembered how she and Joe had stayed up late, helping Mum and Dad fix the tree that Dad had brought over from the park, and trying to wrap up the presents without letting the others see what they had got. She also remembered how Mr and Mrs Grant from next door had come in for a drink, and how they'd all ended up playing charades, and then Mum had sung a song about a nightingale, and Dad had kissed her under the mistletoe hanging above the door, and then they'd all got up and danced, with just the Christmas tree lights on . . .

Ellen was hit by a great feeling of loneliness she had never felt before, and a longing to be back in her own familiar home.

Chapter 5

THE FARM SCHOOL

'Now remember, children, the first thing is the customs, so make sure you've got all your things with you.'

While Mr Morris was speaking, Joe and Ellen gazed down on the mass of people on the dockside. Everyone seemed to be wearing brightly coloured clothes. A band was playing, and in one corner a group of children were jumping up and down, and waving to the ship. Beyond the buildings behind them stood a long brown train, steaming gently in the heat.

'Is that our train?' Joe asked Ellen.

'I expect so,' she replied. 'Aren't they different from the ones in England!'

'Bet they're not as fast!' Joe said, suddenly excited.

As they left the shade of the ship and clattered down the gangplanks, they felt the heat of the sun on their heads.

'I'd forgotten about it being hot!' Ellen said. 'I hope they've got a swimming pool at the school.'

'Me too,' Joe said.

They stepped on to the dock, and followed the rest of the children across the quayside. As they neared the building at the back, they noticed the boys and girls were being sent in different directions.

'Why are they doing that?' Joe asked.

'That's for when we go through the customs,' she replied, not quite sure why they had to do this.

'Oh.'

Ellen heard the anxiety in Joe's voice. 'Don't worry, we'll be able to sit together on the train. First one there saves the other a seat. All right?'

'All right,' Joe replied, uncertainly.

And so they went their separate ways into the building.

Joe was glad to be out of the heat. He noticed there were a lot of boys ahead of him, waiting to have their cases looked at. Even in the Home he'd never seen so many together. After what seemed ages, he reached the front of the queue, and lifted his cases up for the man to see.

'Where are you bound for, fella?' the man boomed out, striking a white cross on the end of his suitcase, and looking down at Joe.

'I'm going to the farm school.'

The man laughed. 'Yeah, but which one?'

'I don't know.'

'Well, where have you come from?'

'The Bethesda Home in London.'

The man looked at a list in front of him. 'OK, you're over in the corner there. See that man in the red cap? He'll sort you out.'

Joe picked up his case, and walked over to where the man had said he should go. The man in the cap was busy talking to a woman. Finally she walked off, and the man turned to the boys around him.

'So you're the London lot?' he said. 'OK, pick up your bags and follow me.' He led them through the back of the building, and over the railway track to the other side of the train. 'OK, anywhere in this carriage. I'll be along soon with your tickets.'

Joe was one of the first to climb aboard. He saved a seat for Ellen by the window. While they waited, he looked at the small, low houses running alongside the track, each with a kind of porch on the front, where people were sitting in the shade. He saw some blue-leaved trees he'd never seen before. And at the edge of the track he noticed a pile of bird cages, each with a brilliantly coloured bird inside, rather like a tiny parrot.

Then Joe realized the train was moving. But it can't be going yet, he thought: what about Ellen? He jumped up, opened the door to the corridor, and ran through to the next carriage. Not there!—nothing but boys in sight. He dashed through to the next one, and ran straight into the man with the red cap.

'Hang on, mate, what's yer hurry?' the man said.

'I'm looking for my sister,' Joe gasped.

'Sister? You'll be lucky, there are no girls on this train.'

'No girls! Why not?' cried Joe, really frightened now.

'Why not?' the man repeated, with a smile. 'Because the girls have gone to the convent school, haven't they? You can't expect them to work on a farm school like you lads.'

Joe was so upset he didn't know what to say. He allowed the man to steer him back to his carriage. Sitting by the window, he tried to think what to do. Should he get off at the next station and try to catch a train back? But then wouldn't Ellen already have left the docks? He could see no way out. But how would he manage without her, amongst all these other boys, and in this strange hot land where people talked so differently?

The sun moved its warmth across Joe's face. He stirred, and slowly opened his eyes. For just a moment he couldn't think where he was. Then he remembered—the separation from Ellen, the long, exhausting journey across strange, flat, red countryside, their arrival in the dark at the farm school, and finally the welcome bed, out in this large building on the farm estate.

He pulled himself up, and looked around the dormitory, still half asleep. His bed was in a corner by the door. Looking down the room, all he could see were beds, beds and more beds. They seemed to go on for ever. Still, he thought, at least there's plenty of space—not like on the boat. He shivered at the memory of that journey.

The next bed to his was several feet away. He saw a head of ginger hair on the pillow. Looking down the row, and then across to the beds on the other side, he realized he was the only one awake. How unlike home! There, he was always the last one up, having to be woken by Ellen. He remembered how she would put their cat next to him on his pillow, and he would be woken by a wet tongue licking his face.

'Hey, new boy!'

From beneath the blankets of one of the beds opposite he saw an arm waving. It stopped, then waved again. Joe swung himself out of bed on to the cold stone floor. It took him a few moments to get used to the chill. Then he walked across to the end of the bed where the hand had come from.

'Sit down!' a voice whispered. A hand came out again from under the blanket, and jabbed a finger at the wooden seat next to the bed. Joe sat down nervously on the chair. There was silence, then the sound of giggling.

'Got no parents, I suppose?' the voice asked, in a different, deeper tone of voice. 'That's nothing to boast about, you know. You're not the only one.'

'But I—' Joe began.

'Don't think I shall be sorry for you, because I won't,' the voice continued, getting louder. 'You're not here to enjoy yourself. Work is our motto on this farm, my lad. You do right by us and we'll do right by you.'

There was silence again. Joe lifted the blanket. As he did so, the dormitory door was thrown open, and a large man came striding in, ringing a handbell, and shouting, 'Let's have you, you lazy kids. Rise and shine like little lambs of hope—if you've got any left, that is!'

When he saw Joe he stopped ringing the bell, and came over to where he was sitting by the boy's bed. His large body blocked out the sun, making it difficult for Joe to see his face.

'And what might you be doing, laddie?'

Joe looked up at the outline of the man's face. 'I was just—I thought . . .' he stammered.

It was hard to find the right words when you didn't

know who you were talking to. Joe realized the other boys had woken up and were watching him. He felt uncomfortable.

'Oh, so that's it, is it?' said the man. He pulled Joe roughly off the chair. 'You're new here, aren't you?'

'Yes I am,' Joe replied, wishing the man wouldn't squeeze his arm so hard.

'Mr Temple to you, my lad, and don't forget it,' the man growled. He pushed Joe out into the space between the two rows of beds. 'Now just get this clear. We're not having any hanky panky in the dormitories—or anywhere else, for that matter. Especially with that idiot Randall there. Understand? I don't know where you were before, and I don't care. But every boy in this school has to stick to the rules. There's quite a lot of rules, but you'll pick them up soon enough—won't he, boys?'

Here the man leered round the dormitory. A few boys answered 'Yes, Mr Temple,' in sleepy voices. Joe at last got a sight of the man's face. He noticed a large mole on his cheek, and his fierce, pale blue eyes. He was dressed in rough clothes, and stood in the middle of the room with his legs apart, holding the bell as if it were a weapon. He turned to Joe again, with a smile that made Joe move backwards towards his own bed.

'I've not finished with you yet, boy,' he said. 'Thought I'd give you a humdinger of a treat on your first day. You can join the water gang, that'll freshen you up for a good day's work. Hawkins! Johnson! Take this little squirt with you. You don't mind getting your nice city clothes dirty, do you, boy?' And with a roar of laughter that echoed round the barn he marched out, the sound of his bell gradually fading into the distance.

At once the room came to life. Boys of different shapes and sizes appeared from under their blankets, leapt out of their beds, and started putting on their clothes at high speed. Anxiously, Joe dragged his small suitcase from under his bed, and struggled to catch up with the others, many of whom were already dressed and leaving the dormitory on the run. The ginger-haired boy next to him was one of the last to be ready.

'Where do we have to go?' Joe asked him anxiously.

'House Two,' the boy replied, running a comb hurriedly through his untidy hair. And he dashed out through the door.

Joe quickly tied his last shoelace, and ran out after him.

When he arrived at House Two, Joe's first job was to collect water from the well, for use in the kitchen. The well was a long way from the main house, and he and Johnson and Hawkins had to make six journeys there and back before the job was finished. Only then were they allowed breakfast.

Unused to the heat of the sun, Joe was already exhausted by eight o'clock. The other two boys said very little. They showed Joe how to work the rope at the well, and where the kitchen was; otherwise they were silent. Joe had remained silent too, though he badly wanted to talk to somebody.

By the time they had finished and got over to House Two, all the others had eaten their breakfast. Although the porridge and the tea were almost cold, and the toast half burnt, Joe was so hot and hungry he hardly noticed. In any case, he only just had time to swallow the last spoonful of porridge before another bell rang.

'What do we have to do now?' he asked the nearest of the two boys. Was it Hawkins or Johnson—he still had no idea who was which?

'It's the bell for the first lesson,' the boy replied. 'If you can call it a lesson.'

Joe soon found out what he meant. As they crossed to the main house, joining up with boys coming from other parts of the farm, he imagined a classroom like the one in London, with rows of neat wooden desks, a nice warm boiler in the corner, a blackboard at one end, and lots of books and pictures on the shelves and walls. Instead, he found a long, low room, quite empty except for a couple of rather old armchairs at one end. The boys all sat on the floor, and talked quietly amongst themselves. Johnson and Hawkins had already drifted away, and Joe was on his own again.

A door at the side of the room opened, and a man came in, holding a bright-green walking-stick. The boys stood up hurriedly, and fell quiet. Joe saw that the man was short and fat, and had a slight limp. He wore glasses, which caught the sunlight as he spoke, flashing circles of light around the walls and into the boys' eyes.

'All right, you can sit,' the man began. 'Now the weather's good again, so it'll be building gangs today. Just as well, you've got a lot of catching up to do. I don't know what's got into you recently—some of you must have gone walkabout.'

He limped to the window, and stood looking out. Then he jerked round suddenly, as if trying to catch someone out. The boys had remained perfectly still.

'Some of the work from the last shift yesterday was bloody useless. Hands up those boys who were on the sand and cement.' Several hands went up. The man frowned. 'Two hours' overtime today for the lot of you. I don't want to see you again until sunset. Now vanish, and show willing. The three new boys, you stay behind.'

Joe was surprised and pleased. He had thought he was the only newcomer. As the boys shuffled unwillingly out of the room, he looked at the other two that remained behind. Do I look as lost and scared as they do, he wondered? Then the man beckoned them across to the armchairs with his stick. He looked closely at each in turn.

'Not a very promising lot. Of course, we don't have any say in the matter. We take what comes, even if it is from the gutter. Everyone gets treated the same here.'

He sat down on the arm of one of the chairs, resting his stick on the other.

'Mr Piggot's my name. From today you're working for me. Got that? If you think this is a hard country, you're not wrong. But a lad can learn a lot from it. Mind you, you only get out what you put in. We don't go in for lessons here. Work is our motto—but we don't have to write it on the blackboard.'

His eyes came to rest on Joe's face.

'You do right by us, we'll do right by you. But anyone not going at it full bore, anyone playing smart—they won't half bloody cop it from me.'

He smashed his stick down on the empty armchair, causing Joe and the others to jump back in alarm. A small cloud of dust rose from the chair, and the man watched it drift towards the window. Then he looked at the boys again.

'Got no parents, I suppose? Well, don't think that makes you anything special here. Everyone's in the same boat, so don't expect me to feel sorry for you. Now, come with me.'

He led them to the door, and pointed into the distance with his green stick. 'See that shack? Just past there is where they're building a new shed for the animals. Go and report to Mr Temple, and he'll set you to work. I want no hanging about, see?'

He limped round the corner of the house, and out of sight.

Joe worked all day on the building. His hands were blistered from the bricks, his back sore from all the lifting and carrying. By noon he could stand the heat of the sun no more. Happily, just then they stopped for their lunch break. One of the bigger boys brought round some bread—each boy was allowed just two slices, together with a small square of cheese, and a mug of cool water.

Joe sat in the shade, and attacked his bread and cheese. He was joined by the ginger-haired boy from the bed next to his. The boy put his peaked cap on the ground, and drained his mug of water in one mouthful.

'You on the new animal shed, then? You're lucky: Piggot put me on the sewage. Worrh, talk about a stink!' He held his nose, and looked sideways at Joe. 'Don't worry, you'll get used to the sun. You ought to get a hat, though.'

Joe looked at him. It was the first time anyone had said anything kind to him. Could this mean a friend at last?

The boy picked up a pebble and threw it in an arc. 'What's your name?' he asked Joe. 'Mine's Tony Anderson, but you can call me Andy if you like. Have you just come from England? What boat did you come on?'

Joe was glad to be able to talk about the last few weeks. The boy listened, chewing on a piece of grass, nodding now and then. He had a round, cheerful face, with a nose covered with freckles, and bunches of ginger hair hanging in a fringe almost over his eyes. Joe was glad they were next to each other in the dormitory.

The whistle blew for the end of the lunch break. 'They don't give you very long, do they? Is the work always as hard as this?' he asked Andy.

His new friend's face became serious. 'That depends what old Pig Face is feeling like,' he said, looking across at the main house. 'He's the one who gives the orders. I hate him, everyone hates him. I'd like to get hold of his stick and break it into pieces and throw it on the fire.' As he got up to go, his face cleared. 'You just have to keep your eyes open for a cloud. If it rains, we get some lessons indoors, if we're lucky. See you at supper.'

He disappeared, and Joe moved slowly back to the site, his heart just a shade lighter than it had been.

At last, in the cool of the evening, Joe was able to rest. The meat at supper had been tough and impossible to eat, so he had had to make do with two boiled potatoes and a bowl of semolina. But by then he hardly cared about the taste of the

59

food. His body was aching all over, and he felt dizzy with tiredness. He had walked across to the barn dormitory where they slept. Nearby, some boys were kicking a ball around a patch of open ground.

Joe sat on a log, half watching the game, and thinking about everything he had seen and done that day. How could he keep going if every day was like today? He had never, ever been so tired in his whole life, nor so miserable.

As the light faded, his mind eased a little. He stood up, and wandered away from the game. In each direction, beyond the fence that ran round the edge of the farm, he saw nothing but bare, parched and flat country, stretching right up to the horizon. There was not a tree to be seen, simply a few scattered bushes. For the first time he realized how far away he was from other people.

As he watched the brilliant red sun drop towards the plain, he wondered where Ellen's new home was, and what she was doing. He hoped she was not having such a hard time as he was. Was she as lonely, he wondered? So much had happened since they had been separated that he had hardly had time to think about her. Now, suddenly, he wished she could be here, making plans for him, helping him in this terrible new life.

Another bell sounded. Joe turned and walked as quickly as he could to the barn. He reached his bed, took off his shoes, climbed under the blanket with all his clothes still on, and was asleep in seconds.

After a month at the farm school, Joe began to get used to the way of life. At least his body did; his mind was a different matter. Every hour of every day he longed to escape.

Sometimes he wondered why it was called a farm *school*, as they hardly ever had any lessons. As long as the weather was good, which it usually was, they worked outside from morning to evening. When it did rain, they were taken into one of the large rooms in House One for lessons. This meant working your way in silence through a book of exercises in English, or one full of sums and long division, while the teacher read a book or magazine. Joe learnt little he didn't already know, and was soon bored.

It also seemed very different from his idea of a farm. Remembering the week he and Ellen had spent in Devon during one summer, Joe had expected to find large herds of cows, dogs, hens, and cats wandering all over the place, and tractors chugging across huge, open fields. Instead there were simply lots of buildings full of sheep, hens and pigs, together with three horses and a foal, which spent most of the day out to pasture in the nearby paddock. There seemed to be no farm machinery in sight, lots of empty open space, and only a few trees or bushes.

Joe began to think the animals had a better life than the boys. He couldn't understand why all the grown-ups were hard, unsmiling men. They seemed to enjoy watching the boys wear themselves out.

Mr Piggot was the worst, with his stick and angry eyes; but the others were nearly as bad. Mr Temple, who had told Joe off that first morning, was the one who kept the closest watch on them on the building site. Often Joe would stop for a rest, only to see Mr Temple's huge, forbidding shadow fall across the ground. He would look up, see his sneering face, and wearily pick up the next load of bricks.

The other staff—the two teachers, and the cook, who came in from the nearby town—all treated the children coldly. The only one who had any time for them was Old Wal, whose job was to run the farm office.

His office was at the back of the main house. It was there that the boys went to collect their pocket-money every Saturday morning, during their lunch break. At least they would have done so if there had ever been any money to collect. But because Mr Temple would keep fining them for being slow at work, or not cleaning the tools properly, they never saw any. Even if they had, Joe soon discovered there was nothing to spend it on.

To begin with Joe thought Wal unfriendly. The first time he went to his office, along with three other boys, Wal looked up, nodded at them, opened his account book, and told each of them how much money they were due, and how much their fines were. Then he ignored them.

The next time Joe came he was by himself. Wal opened his account book as usual, and told Joe his latest position.

'A real scorcher today, isn't it?' he said suddenly.

'Yes,' Joe said, surprised.

Wal took a glass from the windowsill, and drew a jug of water across his battered desk. 'Want some?' he said.

'Oh—yes please,' Joe replied, even more surprised.

Wal passed him the glass, glanced out of the window, and ran his hand through his thin, sandy hair.

'Getting used to it yet?' he said finally.

Joe wasn't sure what to answer.

'Most of 'em do,' Wal went on. 'Not much choice, is there?'

'No,' said Joe carefully. There was something rough but warm about Wal that he liked, with his broad, chunky face, merry blue eyes and deep soft voice.

'Piggot been rough with you, has he?'

'Well—'Joe began.

'It's not my way, treating you like dingoes, belting the living daylights out of you. But there you go, it's not my farm.'

Joe wished it was. But he wondered why Wal stayed here, if he didn't agree with the way the children were treated.

As if reading his mind, Wal added: 'No pension, you see, mate. It gives me some pocket-money.' Then, suddenly angry: 'The stingy bastards! All they want to do is make money.'

After that, Joe came to the office every week. Wal fed him scraps about his life. He told him how he was

62

wounded in the Great War in Europe, in a place called the Dardanelles. He talked about his years mustering cattle as a stockman in the bush. Joe also enjoyed hearing about when he was a barman in a hotel, and stories about the people who lived there. Wal told him he had come to the farm after his wife died: he had been staying in the town nearby when someone in the hotel bar told him there was a job going. 'A man has to keep on the move,' he would say, as if next week he was planning to be off somewhere else.

These chats with Wal were the only moments of relief Joe had. But it wasn't just the work that was getting him down. It was something else, which for a while he didn't understand. It came to him suddenly one morning, as he was walking to the well to fetch the water, and wondering how many journeys like this he would have to make during the year at the farm.

None of the grown-ups here cares one bit what happens to me, he said to himself. Nobody except Wal says anything nice or kind. They just want us to work all the time. I hate it *so* much. If only Ellen was here with me, she'd help me, she'd know what to do. I wish I knew where she was.

As he reached the well he threw the bucket to the ground and, for the first time since he came to the farm, burst into tears.

Chapter 6
THE ORPHANAGE

Even now, Ellen could not believe it had happened. For several hours, the coach rattled along the lonely roads, through the wild and strange landscape. Yet still she could think of nothing but Joe, and their cruel separation only a few hours before.

If only I'd stayed with him, she told herself again. She remembered the long wait at the customs, how uneasy she felt, and then the sound of the train moving out of the station. She had run out into the heat of the sun, only to see the heavy brown train already steaming away. She had run after it, crying out 'Joe! Joe!', but the train had just become smaller and smaller. Soon she had stopped and stood where the train had been a moment before, her tears falling on to the dusty platform.

She could hardly remember the next few minutes. Dimly she recalled a man helping her away, and then two nuns leading her to a coach, saying: 'God will take care of you.' Stunned, she sat numbly in her seat until the coach began its journey.

For several hours she had gazed out of the window, as the coach sped across the salmon-pink land, with its isolated bare trees and endless dry yellow grass. And now, as the late afternoon sun touched the red rocks rising up in the distance, she thought for the first time about what might be in store for her.

Just then the girl in the seat next to her awoke, blinking with the sharpness of the light slanting into the coach.

'Where are we?' she said to Ellen.

'I don't know. I don't know where we're going,' Ellen replied. 'Do you?'

'I think Sister said it was called Our Lady,' the girl said, yawning. At the front Ellen saw the back of two nuns' habits flapping to the rhythm of the coach.

'Is it a religious place, then?' Ellen said, puzzled.

'Of course it is, silly!' the girl said, laughing. She looked at Ellen. 'You *are* a Catholic, aren't you?'

'No,' Ellen replied.

'What are you then?

'I'm not anything.'

'That's funny.'

Ellen thought so, too, but decided she'd better say no more.

After her first week at Our Lady of the Assumption, Ellen felt angry, miserable and trapped. Was this really going to be her home for the next year?

For a while, during the first morning, when she and the other new girls were being shown round, she had been hopeful. Compared to the Home, the orphanage seemed a friendly place. It was small, so it was easy to find your way around. Everything seemed clean and white and shining, instead of the gloom and shabbiness of Bethesda. In each room they looked into there seemed to be sun coming through the windows. Ellen especially liked the garden in the middle of the building, with its wooden seats, and its beds full of flowers she had never seen before.

But she soon realized there was more to her new home than light and sunshine. Later that morning all the new girls were summoned to the chapel, to meet Reverend Mother. As they filed nervously in, Ellen wondered how she would remember the names of the nuns. In their black outfits and funny pointed white hats they all looked the same.

A bell rang, and Reverend Mother came in from the back of the chapel. As she walked down the aisle, Ellen noticed how small she was, how delicate her hands were as she held them in front of her. But when she started speaking from the altar steps, Ellen heard a voice surprisingly deep and powerful.

'Good morning, dear children,' she boomed, her words echoing round the chapel. 'I humbly welcome you to our Order. I hope you will find here the comfort and the joy that have been missing from your lives. It pleases me greatly that God has seen fit to send you across the world in order that you may live amongst us, and strive with us to do His bidding.'

She stopped, overtaken by a heavy fit of coughing; Ellen noticed the candles nearest to her flicker, as if they were scared of her breath. She recovered, and looked round at the girls.

'The life we lead is a simple one,' she continued. 'You will, of course, be treated in exactly the same way as our own girls: we are all equal in the sight of the Lord. But you will not find it easy: the road to perfection is hard and rocky, and fraught with dangers and temptations. So in your daily lives we look for an obedience that will make you worthy of our Holy Mother.' She coughed again. 'And now we will ask our dear Lord to forgive us for all our sins.'

During the prayer, which she couldn't understand, Ellen looked around. All the other girls had their heads bowed, but she couldn't bring herself to do the same. After all, she didn't believe in God, did she? Then she noticed a girl with fair hair and plaits, who was also sitting up straight. The girl saw Ellen at the same moment, and gave a small shrug of the shoulders, as if to say, 'What can we do?'

After the prayer was finished, the girls were told which Sister would be responsible for them, and which classes they would be in. They then had a few minutes of spare time before lunch. Ellen managed to catch up with the fair-haired girl in the corridor.

'Hello, I'm Ellen,' she said.

'Oh, well, I'm Lizzie,' the girl replied, with an open, friendly smile.

'Why are you here?' Ellen asked.

'Because my parents are dead, and my foster parents moved to America,' she replied.

Ellen suddenly felt a bit ashamed that her own parents were alive. 'Did you want to come to Australia?' she asked Lizzie.

'Not really. But they said there was no room in the children's home near us.'

'Are you a Catholic?'

'No—and you aren't either, are you?' Lizzie replied. 'I could tell. What should we do?'

'Just tell one of the Sisters, I suppose. Then we won't have to go to chapel.'

'I hope not. You have to go three times a day.'

'Three times! How do you know that?'

'I heard the Australian girls talking at breakfast.'

Ellen thought for a moment. 'Whose group are you in?'

Lizzle giggled. 'She's called Sister Winterbottom. What a name, eh? She was on the coach yesterday.'

'What's she like?'

'I think she's pretty strict. Why?'

'I was thinking, perhaps we could go and tell someone like her together?'

'All right,' said Lizzie, cheerfully. 'That will make it easier.' They walked on together, Ellen relieved to have found a friend. 'We're supposed to meet her after lunch at half past one, in her room there, the next one on the left— oh, maybe she's there now. Shall we see?'

Ellen suddenly felt nervous. 'All right,' she said.

Lizzie knocked. A voice asked them to enter. They found themselves in a small classroom, with desks in neat rows. At one end a nun was busy writing on the blackboard. They stood uneasily, waiting for her to finish. Finally she turned round.

'Well, my children?' she said, crossly.

'Please, Sister, we want to talk to you about going to chapel,' Ellen began.

'You know how to get there, don't you?' Sister Winterbottom said. 'If not, you soon will, child.'

'No, what I mean is—'Ellen looked at Lizzie.

Lizzie took a deep breath. 'You see, Sister, we're not really Catholic children, so we thought, would it be all right if we did something else while the other girls were going to the services, like . . .?' Her words tailed off as she saw Sister's face turn to a scowl.

'Not really Catholic children—how can you say such a thing, my child?'

'But we're not, we never have been!' Lizzie burst out. 'There must have been a mistake.'

'That is not a matter for us to decide,' Sister replied. She looked at the chalk in her hand. 'There is a purpose in everything God does, though we may not understand it at the time.'

'Yes, but—' Ellen began.

'I think it would be best if I took you to see Reverend Mother,' Sister said firmly. 'Come with me.'

Sitting in her highbacked chair in her small, very bare sitting-room, Reverend Mother listened to what Ellen and Lizzie had to say. Then, with a bang that made Ellen jump, she closed the book that had been open on her lap.

'I don't think you understand, my children,' she said. 'You are among the lucky ones that Our Lord has chosen. Back in your own country, you had nothing to look forward to but neglect and suffering. Here you have a chance of a new life, a new beginning.'

She rose from the chair, and stood close to them. Ellen felt she wanted to back away. 'There are not many places that would offer you shelter and support as we have done. That is why you are here. In the past we have opened our doors to children who do not yet share our faith, in the belief that they would in due course want to follow our path. Some have done so; perhaps you will join them before long?'

She looked at each girl in turn. 'But first you will need to be humble, to submit your minds and bodies to God, and learn wisdom from those around you. And now, my children, I have work to do. The blessings of the Lord be upon you.' And she moved to a desk in the corner.

As they walked down the corridor, the two girls were silent. Then Lizzie spoke: 'They can make us do things, but they can't tell us what to think, can they?' she said fiercely.

'No, they can't,' Ellen agreed.

The next day, Ellen had another unpleasant surprise. At breakfast, she and the other dozen new English girls were asked to return to their dormitory. There they found two of the Sisters.

'Just find a place on one of these beds,' one of them said. 'All right. Now, I'm Sister Veronica, and I'm in charge of the domestic arrangements. First things first: your clothes. Sister Frances?'

The other Sister wheeled a rack of dark green dresses and jerseys into the middle of the room. 'These are your uniforms,' Sister Veronica continued. 'They have been handed down as other girls have grown out of them. There is nothing showy or vulgar about them. They reflect the simple life we lead here, under the guidance of our Holy Mother. In this way, no girl has an advantage over her neighbour.'

She began to walk slowly up and down between the two rows of beds. 'The uniforms are to be worn at all times, except when you are doing your chores, when overalls will be worn. You will get those this afternoon. Meanwhile, I want you to make a pile of your outer clothes, and leave them on your bed. They will be kept for you until you leave here.'

There was an uneasy silence. Ellen felt unhappy at the idea

69

of having to give up her clothes, and she was sure the others felt the same. 'Please, would it be all right if we kept them in our cases under the bed?' she asked.

'No, child, we don't want to leave temptation in your way. A rule is a rule. Now, each choose a dress and a jersey that is about your size, and then try it on behind those screens at the end of the dormitory. Then, once you have put out your other clothes, remain on your bed, and Sister Frances will come round and cut your hair.'

'But I don't want my hair cut, I *like* it long!' one girl said, looking very unhappy.

'So do I,' said another, clutching at one of her plaits.

'Quiet this moment!' said Sister Veronica. 'These rules have been made for your own good. This is not the kind of behaviour we expect here: you should be grateful that the Lord has seen fit to offer you shelter with us. We will have silence while you choose your uniforms.'

Ellen found a dress about the right size for her. She noticed the other girls were less lucky. Lizzie, being rather small, had to make do with one much too long for her. A fat girl couldn't fit into any of them, and was told she would have to wait until some alterations were made.

But the worst moment was the haircutting. Ellen's hair was short anyway, so she minded less than others did. But several girls were very upset, and cried once it had been done. When it came to the turn of the girl with the plaits, she struggled desperately and screamed out 'No! No!' She had to be held down by Sister Veronica while the scissors were used. When it was over, Sister Veronica told them they could stay in the dormitory until lunch, so that they could get used to their new appearance.

As soon as the Sisters left, the girls all started talking at once. Lizzie came and sat next to Ellen.

'I'd like to kill those two nuns!' she said. 'Do I look very stupid? It feels horrible!'

'I think it might quite suit you,' Ellen replied, though she wasn't sure if it would. 'What about mine?'

'Yours doesn't look much different. I feel sorry for Millie though.'

Ellen looked over to where the girl with the plaits sat on her bed, her head in her hands. Seeing her and the others with their hair cropped so close, she was suddenly reminded of a newsreel she'd seen towards the end of the war, showing Polish children standing sadly in the street, their hair cut short. One of them, she remembered, looked rather like Joe. She went and sat next to Millie, and put her arm around her.

Over the next few days, Ellen felt increasingly helpless. Life at the orphanage seemed to be nothing but work, study and prayer. This was hard enough for the English girls who *were* Catholic; for Ellen it was almost unbearable, being so unlike anything she had known before.

They had to get up at six in the morning in order to go to mass. For the first few days, she and Lizzie were allowed to sit together at the side of the chapel, and watch the service. But they had to have special religious instruction and learn the catechism every day in the middle of the morning, while the other girls had a break. Then, after tea and again before bedtime, all the girls had to return to the chapel for further services.

Ellen began to hate that chapel, with its dark wooden pews, narrow windows, and the sickly smell of incense hanging in the air. Unlike the rest of the orphanage, it never got any proper light, even though the sun was almost always shining. It seemed such a miserable place. She wondered why everything to do with God seemed to be like that.

Most of the girls were Australian, and from their first day they teased the English girls, laughing at their different accents, their ill-fitting uniforms, and their tightly cropped hair.

On the third day, Ellen was walking down the corridor

71

with Lizzie. As they drew close to a group of Australian girls, the tall one in front called out 'Baldy-pom! Baldy-pom!' The others burst out laughing. Lizzie turned round and slapped the girl round the head. At once the two of them were wrestling on the ground, the Australian girls cheering on their friend.

At that moment Sister Clare came hurrying up. 'What is going on?' she shouted. 'Stop that at once, do you hear?' She pulled the two girls apart. 'Audrey, what is your explanation for all this?' she asked the tall girl.

'She just hit me, for nothing,' Audrey replied, straightening her dress.

'That's a lie!' Lizzie burst in. 'You know—'

'That will do!' Sister Clare interrupted, her face red with anger. 'You know such behaviour is totally forbidden by Reverend Mother.' She looked around. 'All of you report to my room immediately after lunch.' And she swept off.

The punishment was immediate and unpleasant. That same evening the girls were forced to kneel on the hard, green-tiled floor of the big bathroom for three hours, and forbidden to move or say a word. One of the Sisters, sitting on a chair nearby with a book, kept watch over them.

As she knelt, her knees and thighs aching with the effort, Ellen felt angry at the unfairness of it all. She also wondered what it had to do with the love of God that the Sisters were always telling them about. She looked across to Lizzie kneeling at the other end of the large bathroom, and saw her give a quick wave. Ellen waved back, and thought to herself: I like Lizzie, she's not afraid of anyone.

The next day was Saturday, the one day the girls were allowed out of the orphanage—though not on their own.

Ellen was uncertain whether to join the group, who were planning to walk to the local creek. She felt unhappy with her uniform and haircut, and hated the idea of people looking at her. But she was curious to find out what sort of place they were living in. She knew they were in a town, but it had been dark and late when the coach arrived that first evening, and all she had wanted to see then was her bed. Since then there hadn't been a chance to leave the building. Now, when she discovered Lizzie was going, she decided she would too.

They were taken by three of the Sisters, who hustled them into pairs on the porch, and made sure each of the new girls had one of the sun hats that were kept in the hall. They then led the girls in a crocodile through the town, which seemed quite small and, to Ellen, rather pretty. She noticed most of the houses and shops were made of wood, like the garden shed back home, only painted grey and pink. People were busy shopping, or leaning against the pillars at the end of the verandahs, talking. She was surprised that nobody took much notice of them, except a few older women, who greeted the Sisters as they passed.

They wound off the main street and into the open. The sky was a deep blue, and cloudless. After the coach journey, where the land seemed to be dry and dead, Ellen was surprised to find they were walking amongst trees and green grass and shrubs. She could feel the sun burning through her thin cotton dress, but when they arrived at the creek there was shade along the water's edge.

'We shall stay an hour,' Sister Emilia said, spreading out a rug for the three adults. 'You may wander a little way, but not out of our sight. I will blow my whistle when it is time to go.'

The Australian girls spread out: one group started a ball game, another sat beneath a low, spreading tree with a thick silver trunk, which offered the best shade in sight. The English girls stood apart, watching. Eventually Lizzie and Ellen moved away, and sat on the bank of the creek. They watched the brightly coloured birds playing on the deep, clear-blue water, and Ellen found herself relaxing for the first time since they had arrived in Australia.

'It's lovely, isn't it,' she said, half to herself.

73

'Yes; but the rest of it is horrible!' Lizzie replied fiercely. She threw a pebble into the water, and watched the circles move out from where it dropped. 'We've got to get away.'

'Yes, but how? Where would we go?' Ellen said.

'Anywhere but this place. They can't keep us here—especially when we're not Catholic. We'll have to complain to someone.'

'But how, Lizzie?'

'I've been thinking. If we could find out where Miss Reed is—you remember, the woman on the ship. Well, we could tell *her* about the mistake, and then she could find somewhere else for us.'

'Yes,' Ellen said, suddenly eager. 'Maybe she could tell me where Joe is, and then we could be in the same place after all. But how are we going to find her?'

'I've thought of that. There must be a letter somewhere, when they arranged for us to come here. If we can find that, it will have Miss Reed's address on, and we can write to her secretly.'

'But where will it be?'

'Probably in Reverend Mother's study. Remember she had that big desk in the corner? That's probably where it is. Miss Reed would write to her, wouldn't she? We'd have to find a way of getting into her room.'

'But supposing we get caught?' Ellen said, anxiously.

'It can't be any worse than it is now, can it?'

'No,' Ellen agreed.

'The best time would be at night, so long as she doesn't lock it. Was there a bed in her room?'

'I don't think so.'

'Nor do I. She must sleep somewhere else.'

'Let's try tonight,' Ellen said, suddenly hopeful.

Lizzie had managed to change beds with another girl, to be next to Ellen. It was hard to stay awake, so they took it in turns. Finally, Lizzie shook Ellen yet again.

'I think we could try it now,' she whispered.

'Are you sure?' Ellen murmured, wanting to go back to sleep.

'Yes, it's quiet downstairs: I went and listened.'

They got dressed, tiptoed past the beds full of sleeping girls, and into the corridor. There were no lights on, but plenty of moonlight to show them the way. They crept slowly along the corridors. Ellen suddenly remembered another night during the war, when she and Joe had watched through the window as the English planes flew across the moon on their way to Germany. How long ago and far away that night seemed! I wonder what Joe is doing now, she thought?

They reached Reverend Mother's room. Lizzie put her ear to the door, and listened. Then she very slowly turned the door knob. The door opened. They moved into the room, Ellen shutting the door gently behind them. The moon shone directly on to the desk, and a filing cabinet next to it, which Lizzie opened.

'This is where she keeps her letters,' she whispered. 'Where do you think it would be?'

'Oh, what's the name of the Society?' Ellen said. 'It was on the notice outside the Home.'

Lizzie worked her way through the files: 'Business, Catering, Damages . . . oh, what about this: England!' She pulled out a mauve file, and sat at the desk, looking through the papers. Then she stopped. 'Here it is—the Fairlane Children's Society.' She began to read it. 'It's a report, I think.'

'But has it got the address on?' Ellen said impatiently.

'What . . . oh, yes, but listen to this. "I am afraid we are not very happy about the latest group of children we are sending you. Their standards of dress and behaviour are low, and most of them come from very poor stock. The war of course is partly to blame. Even so, we must discuss with London how this can be avoided in the future. We must pick and choose more carefully, to make sure that the type of child who comes is a credit to the Society, and not a blot on its name."'

They looked at each other for a moment. 'Do you think that means us?' Ellen whispered.

'I don't know,' Lizzie replied. 'But it's horrible, isn't it? People can't help who their parents are.'

'No, they can't,' Ellen agreed, seeing in her mind a picture of Dad lying on the stretcher. Then she remembered where they were. 'Quick, write down the name and address!'

Lizzie found a pencil and some paper in the desk, and scribbled them down. She put the paper in her dress pocket, returned the file to the cabinet, and straightened the desk. They left the room quickly and silently. Ellen was excited: at last there was a chance of freedom! Then, as they climbed the stairs leading to their dormitory, she saw the outline of a figure at the top. She stopped and clutched Lizzie's arm.

'Please continue your journey!' said a quiet voice. They reached the top of the stairs, and met Sister Veronica.

'So, it's you two again. And where exactly have *you* been?'

'We've . . . we were suddenly hungry, we thought we might find some bread in the kitchen,' Lizzie managed to get out.

'I see. And that is how you show us your gratitude, is it? By breaking the night-time rules, and trying to deprive others of what the Lord has provided for them? Very well. Return to your beds immediately, and report to my room after chapel in the morning. This is not a matter to be treated lightly.'

They returned to the dormitory, and climbed into bed. After a while Lizzie leaned across. 'I don't care. We got what we wanted, didn't we? Here, I've memorized the address, just in case. You better as well.'

Ellen took the piece of paper, and did so.

The room was empty, except for the chair that Ellen sat on, and a picture of Mary and the baby Jesus on the wall.

She tried to hold back her tears, but the pain was still too much. She looked down at her hands, at the deep red marks lying across her palms. She thought nothing had hurt her so much in all her life.

But it wasn't just the pain itself; it was the way they had been given the punishment that morning. Ellen remembered most the eyes of the other girls upon her, as she and Lizzie stood in front of them at breakfast time, while Reverend Mother spoke.

'I am deeply shocked at such conduct, and in such a short time after your arrival here,' she began. 'Do not think that you will get away with breaking the rules simply because you are newcomers. Your behaviour has offended and upset all the Sisters, who work so hard to look after the welfare of the girls.'

Here she picked up a long leather stick from the table. 'And so we have to chastise you, however painful this may be to us. This is why you will go without breakfast today. This is why, once you have taken your punishment, you will sit for the rest of the morning on your own, so that you may search your hearts and come to understand the error of your ways. Now, your hand please, child.'

Ellen knew the Australian girls were waiting to see if she would cry. As she tensed herself for the blow, she caught sight of Reverend Mother's face, her lips drawn tightly together in a thin smile. Then the stick came down on her hand, and she felt the sudden, slicing pain. Again and again the stick cut sharply into her skin. By the tenth blow she was crying out in agony: 'Stop! Please stop!' Finally it was over. She sank on to a chair in the corner of the classroom.

Now it was Lizzie's turn. Through her tears, Ellen saw her friend turn away, as Reverend Mother raised the stick to her. Ellen turned away too, and heard only the noise of the blows. From Lizzie she heard no sound at all. When it was over Ellen looked back. Lizzie's face was white and still. The other girls were watching her. She turned to Reverend Mother: 'Thank you,' she said and, gripping her hands tightly, came and sat next to Ellen.

Later, after the three hours on their own, Ellen and Lizzie sat together on one of the garden seats.

'Does it still hurt?' Lizzie said.

'Not quite so much,' Ellen replied. 'What about yours?'

'Still stinging. But listen, Ellen: do you think you could stand it again?'

'What do you mean?'

'I've had another idea. Perhaps we could get ourselves expelled. Just go on breaking the rules until they throw us out.'

'Do you think they would?'

'If we did it a lot, they might. It's worth trying, isn't it?'

'But what about the letter?'

'I was thinking about that this morning. Perhaps it *wasn't* a mistake us being sent here. Perhaps they meant to do it. But I suppose we could still try writing.'

Ellen was wondering if they would ever escape. What else can we do? she thought, as she moved slowly round the chapel on her knees, polishing and waxing the wooden floor.

She had been given the job as a punishment after she and Lizzie had been caught whispering during prayers. She had been working now for two hours, and it was hurting her knees and her back. But such things hardly bothered her any more.

Over the last three weeks, she and Lizzie had got into trouble many times. They had been beaten, put in isolation, made to clean the lavatories, forbidden to go on outings, and forced to do many dirty, unpleasant jobs. But still they had gone on misbehaving. After a while, even though the punishments continued, the Sisters stopped giving them lectures about how God would punish them.

Ellen had thought quite a lot about God during this time. She was even more sure now that there was no such person. If there had been, she thought, how could he possibly allow me and Lizzie to be here, when we've done nothing wrong? And why would he let people like Sister Veronica go on about being loving and merciful, when they seemed to enjoy hitting children?

Just then she heard the organ start to play at the back of the chapel. There was something odd about the music—and then she recognized the tune of 'God Save the King'. She stood up, and saw it was Lizzie playing. She dropped her cloth, and ran down the aisle to the organ.

'What are you doing?' she asked.

'I'm celebrating!' Lizzie replied.

'What for?'

'No more Latin, no more French—and no more Reverend Mother!'

'What do you mean?' said Ellen.

Lizzie's eyes were glowing. 'We're free, Ellen! We're free!'

'What! How do you know? Tell me, tell me!'

'Miss Reed is coming to collect us this afternoon. We have to pack our things and get ready. Sister Angelica sent me to tell you. We've won, Ellen, we've beaten them!' And she played a loud crashing chord on the organ.

Ellen was hardly able to believe the news. 'Are you sure it's not some trick?' she said.

'Of course I am, silly. They just want to get rid of us. Come on, you can forget all about that stupid polishing now.'

Ellen ran down the aisle to collect the cleaning things. She looked over to the altar for a moment. 'Perhaps you *are* real after all,' she whispered. And she ran back to Lizzie.

But it was only after they had packed and changed into

their own clothes and said goodbye to the other girls, and seen a dark blue car draw up in the road outside, that Ellen really believed they were leaving.

Miss Reed greeted them, and asked them to wait while she spoke with Reverend Mother. After a few minutes she returned, frowning.

'I gather you have caused Reverend Mother a great deal of pain and distress with your poor behaviour,' she said. 'You can hardly be surprised that they have asked me to find you an alternative home.'

'But it's a *horrible* place,' Ellen said angrily. 'All they ever want—'

'Now that's quite enough from you, young lady. The Sisters are doing a marvellous job here under extremely difficult conditions, and all you can do is complain. Not to mention the precious time I'm having to spend, finding you somewhere to live.'

After that Ellen kept silent, realizing they depended on Miss Reed to get them out. There would be plenty of time once she was settled in a happier place to tell her about the orphanage.

A few minutes later, having exchanged brief farewells with Reverend Mother, with Miss Reed standing by them, the two girls walked out of the door, and climbed into the car that would take them to freedom. Ellen settled into the back seat alongside Lizzie, and took a last look at the house of God that had caused them so much pain and misery.

Chapter 7

A HARD LIFE

Since that first day, Joe had become friends with Andy. Although he was two years older than Joe, he didn't seem to mind spending time with him. For Joe it was like having an older brother, who could show you everything, or tell you who to watch out for.

Joe found this friendship useful. Life on the farm was hard for a new boy. The food was always the same, and there was never enough of it. You had to wash your own clothes in the laundry shed, and clean out the lavatories in turn. You also had to learn how to cope with other boys, some of whom seemed almost as cruel as the staff. In his first week Joe and the other new boys were grabbed by a group of them, and taken down to the pig shed, where their heads were forced down into the pigswill.

Luckily, Andy seemed to be better than most boys at keeping out of trouble. This meant that Joe managed to do so too. Having someone like this to rely on was very important, for Joe quickly realized how hard it was to avoid being punished. There were so many rules, it seemed impossible *not* to break at least one a week, even when you didn't know you were doing so.

There were really only two punishments you could get: extra work on the estate, or a beating. Two of the older boys, Ken and John, were always getting into trouble. Whenever Joe saw them they seemed to be laughing, joking or shouting. They were brothers from Liverpool, and some of the staff, like Mr Temple, would pick on them, and tease them about their accent. This made them angry, they would shout back, and end up getting the stick or slipper from Mr Piggot.

Andy told Joe that this had been going on ever since he had come to the farm, and that the beatings didn't make any difference to what the brothers did. Joe knew he wouldn't be so brave. Luckily, so far he had only had to do extra labouring as a punishment.

One afternoon, as Joe and Andy were cleaning out the pig house, they heard shouting in the distance. They went outside, and saw a small crowd gathering by the building site. Several boys were running in that direction from different parts of the estate.

'Come on!' Andy yelled, already on his way.

When they reached the site, they found a ring of cheering boys, and in the middle three bodies rolling around in the dust.

'It's Temple!' Andy called out, his eyes shining.

The bodies were thrashing around so much, and creating so much dust, it was a moment before Joe realized it was Ken and John fighting with Mr Temple.

'How did it start?' he asked a boy next to him.

'John dropped a hod of bricks, and Temple called him a stupid Pom,' he replied, keeping his eyes on the fight. 'Then Ken just hit him. Good, isn't it!'

Just then four adults burst through the circle, broke into the fight, and pulled the two brothers clear. The watching boys went silent as Mr Temple rose slowly to his feet, his face cut and bruised, his shirt torn. He looked at Ken and John with hatred.

'You'll wish you'd never been born when I've finished with you,' he growled, trying to recover his breath. 'Bring them over to House One: Mr Piggot will have plenty to say about this.' The boys, still breathing heavily, were taken away. Mr Temple looked around the circle, taking in every face. 'Don't think you scum will get off free,' he shouted. 'Get back to your work!' And he strode out through the circle.

Supper was never much of a meal, but that evening the boys got nothing but bread and milk. Afterwards Mr Piggot and Mr Temple, together with the staff who had broken up the fight, came into the dining-room. The boys fell quiet as Mr Piggot scowled behind his glasses, and beat his green stick softly against his side.

'So, battle is joined, eh?' he said. 'Suits me, suits me down to the ground. All right you two, out front.'

As Ken and John got off their bench, he looked slowly round the room. Joe felt his skin go prickly with fear. Mr Piggot spoke softly.

'Now, if it's not too much trouble for you lads, I'd like a few witnesses. Some of you obviously enjoyed the spectacle this afternoon. I'd hate you to miss the return match. In fact, I'm not giving you any choice. We know exactly who was there. Stand up, the lot of you.'

There was a pause. Then boys started to get to their feet. Joe saw Andy get up, and he did so as well. Mr Piggot smiled sourly.

'Well, well, what obedient little boys. Your parents must have done a good job after all. Oh but I'm forgetting, you don't have parents, do you? What bad luck.' He turned to the other staff. 'All right, I want four of you to take the two ringleaders to the shower room. We'll join you in a minute.'

Ken and John were led out. Mr Piggot leant against the wall, lit a cigarette, and waited. No one dared to move. Joe heard a bird singing outside the window. After what seemed a very long while one of the staff returned, and nodded at Mr Piggot. He stubbed out the cigarette on the back of a chair.

'OK, let's go and see the show. I'm sure you'd like to have front-row seats. Those of you standing, follow me.'

The long, open room had five showers in it. Joe and the others were made to stand opposite the showers, each of which had one of the staff standing by the taps. At the end of the room Joe saw Ken and John, naked and shivering.

Next to them was Mr Temple. Joe noticed he had a stick.

'All right, Mr Temple,' Mr Piggot said. 'The floor is yours. And I want you other boys to watch carefully. Remember, this could well be you next time.'

The first shower was turned on, and Mr Temple prodded Ken under it. He shivered as the cold water ran down his body. Then the lever was suddenly switched to hot. He screamed out in pain and leapt away from the water. As he did so Mr Piggot and Mr Temple held him against the wall, and took it in turn to beat him on the backside with their sticks, calling out numbers as they did so, all the way to ten. Then they pushed him under the next shower, and the treatment started all over again.

Joe wanted to look away, but found he couldn't. The steam started to build up in the room. 'Four!' Every time a blow fell on Ken, he felt his own body shake. 'Five!' Joe began to feel light in the head. Ken's screams got louder and louder. 'Six!' Joe looked down to where John was standing, and saw him clutching his body. 'Seven!' He looked back at Ken, and saw the deep red marks on his body. 'Eight!' Dimly he saw Mr Temple's arm raised high through the steam, to strike again. 'Nine!' At that moment he passed out.

When Joe came round he found he was sitting outside the shower room, with one of the staff trying to revive him. His head felt heavy, his clothes were wet, and he felt sick. Worst of all, he could still hear the screams of pain coming from the showers. He was taken back to the dining-room, where the other boys were still sitting.

For a while afterwards he dreamed every night of what he had seen and heard. The dreams were all mixed up and different, but Mr Temple was always there, with a stick much bigger than the actual one he used. And whatever was happening in the dream, Joe could hear Ken's screams, at first quiet in the background, then becoming louder and more and more unbearable—until Joe would wake up, shaking and covered with sweat.

The incident shocked and upset all the boys. They said little about it to those who had not been there. Strangely, Ken and John seemed to be less affected than the others. Although they were in bed for a couple of days, once they were up they were joking and laughing again—though Joe noticed it didn't happen so often.

Joe knew he would never be able to stand such a punishment. And from this moment he began to think seriously about escaping. He wondered if any other boys had tried. One afternoon, as he and three others sat in the shade at the end of the day's work, he put the question to Andy.

'Yes, there have been a few,' his friend said.

'Tell me,' Joe said, eagerly.

Andy looked down at his hands. Joe saw the scratches left by the rough bricks, and felt the sting in his own palms.

'There was Jamie Price,' Andy said.

'What did he do?'

'It was before I came, but Jimmy told me about it. He'd been beaten by Piggot, lots of times. One night he told Jimmy he was going to leave. After lights out he just got up, put on his clothes, and walked out into the bush.'

'What, you mean without any food or anything?'

'Yes. Jimmy tried to give him some money he'd stolen from Old Wal's office, but he wouldn't have it. We never saw him again.'

'What happened to him?'

'They think he probably died out there.'

Joe stared out across the dry, red earth beyond the edge of the farm. He'd never seen such space before. At the far horizon the hills were softening to pale blue in the late afternoon. He shivered at the idea of being alone in such a place. He wondered how far Jamie had got.

Andy interrupted his thoughts: 'The best one was Sam, when he escaped last Christmas.' He laughed.

85

'He was really clever, he hid in the back of the Blitz truck.'

'What's that?'

'The truck that brings the food in once a month. He climbed in one of the empty packing boxes at the last moment. Ray and me made sure the driver didn't notice. We pretended to have a fight just as he was leaving, right by the truck. He came round to try and stop us, and Sam got into the back. It was really good!'

'And they didn't catch him?'

'No. He got work on a cattle station further north. That's what Old Wal told us.'

Joe kicked the dust hard in front of him. 'That's what I'm going to do then,' he said firmly. 'When does the truck come next?'

'Don't bother!' Andy said.

'Why not?'

'Because now they take the register just before the truck goes, and we're kept in the classroom till it's gone.'

Joe sighed. For a moment there had seemed a chance to get away.

The next day, when Joe arrived in Wal's office for his weekly chat, he found him chuckling to himself.

'They'll be on their best behaviour now,' he said, tapping his pen cheerfully on his desk.

'What do you mean?' Joe asked him.

'Time for the check-up. The man from the Society; he always comes about now, to see if the place passes muster. Puts the flaming fear of God in them!'

'What Society?'

'The people that sent you lot over here, for the good of your health—I *don't* think. They have to keep an eye, you know, make sure everything's happy on the homestead—ha!'

'What does he do, this man?' Joe asked.

'Not much. He gets shown around, asks a few questions,

gets his tucker, goes off to write his report, and no one's any the wiser. At least you'll be all right for one day. He's no drongo, is Piggot: butter wouldn't melt in his mouth when the inspector's here.'

Joe had an idea. 'Does he inspect girls' schools as well? Perhaps he'll know where my sister is?'

'Possibly. But he won't tell you if he does.'

'Why not?'

'These blokes like to keep the boys and girls separate from each other—they reckon they work harder.'

'But she's my *sister*!' Joe cried out, angrily.

Wal frowned. 'Don't blame me, mate: I didn't make the rules.'

Just then another boy came in, and Joe left. But the thought of the inspection jostled around in his mind all day. This is my chance! he thought to himself. And if the man doesn't know where Ellen is, perhaps he'll know someone who does?

Joe wondered how he would get a chance to talk to the inspector. Andy suggested the best bet would be at lunchtime. The inspector was usually invited to sit with some of the older boys, but Andy said he should be able to catch him on his way out.

As the day came closer, Joe became nervous and excited. The hours seemed longer than ever. At night he kept waking and thinking about Ellen, and the fact that he might see her soon. Then, the day before the inspection, he woke with a severe headache. He tried to behave normally, but he knew he wasn't well. Immediately after breakfast he was violently sick, right in front of the kitchen window. The cook came out, and took him to the sick room. Another boy was sent to get his pyjamas and sponge bag, and he was put to bed.

By evening he was still weak and had a temperature, and found he didn't want any food. I *must* get better for tomorrow, he told himself, realizing there was nothing he could do about it. He went to sleep fearing the worst.

In the morning he did feel better, but he still had a temperature. The cook came in with breakfast, saying he might be able to get up in the afternoon. But Joe knew this was no good; Andy had said the inspector always left straight after lunch.

He heard voices outside his window, and got up to see what was happening. Mr Piggot and Mr Temple were below. Mr Temple was pointing out across the land. Following his arm, Joe saw a trail of red dust creeping across the plain. A few minutes later a small, black, very dirty car pulled up. As Joe looked down from his window, a tall, white-faced man stepped out, and shook hands with Mr Piggot and Mr Temple. Then the men disappeared into the house.

Joe noticed the car was the same model that Dad used to drive during the war—an Austin something, he remembered vaguely. For a moment he was back in England. He recalled the smell of the leather on the back seat when the sun shone on it, and how comfortable it was. Even when Dad had given him a ride in the boot through the park, it was still . . . Then the idea came to him. Of course, the boot!

He felt his heart beating faster. He went and lay down, trying to think clearly. He knew there was plenty of room in there . . . if he could just choose the right moment . . . maybe when they were all having lunch? He thought about the position of the car. It was parked at the end of the building, well out of sight of the dining-room. I could slip out of the side door, and make a run for it, he thought. He looked round the room. On the chair were the clothes he was wearing when he fell sick. The rest of his belongings were in the barn: how would he get them?

By the end of the morning he had his plan worked out. When the cook came he pretended to be sleepy. 'Do you want lunch or don't you?' she said, clearly in a hurry.

'No, thank you,' Joe said. 'I think I'll sleep this afternoon; I don't feel like getting up yet.'

'Right then.' She picked up his breakfast tray, and left.

Joe waited a couple of minutes, then moved quickly. He took a look out of the window. The farm grounds were empty. Everyone must be at lunch, he thought. He put on his clothes, grabbed his pyjamas and sponge bag, crept to the door, and opened it.

He could hear the noise of plates and cutlery from the kitchen below. Carefully he edged his way down the back stairs to the back door, which was already open.

He looked round, aware again of the heat after his hours inside. No one was in sight. He ran the few yards to the nearest outhouses. He moved warily round the back, well covered from anyone looking out of the main building. He scurried along the side, disturbing a sheep that was lying in the shade of the iron roof. Under cover of the barn sheds and huts he finally reached the barn.

He thought quickly, then made up his mind. I'll just take my smaller suitcase in case I have to run, he said to himself. He pushed as many clothes as would fit into the battered brown case.

He pulled his other suitcase out from under the bed, and took out an envelope holding three small photos—one each of Mum and Dad and Ellen. He slipped them inside the case, together with his Chelsea football badge. The case was now full. Joe paused. Then he looked under Andy's bed, pulled out a green case, and quickly pushed the remaining clothes inside it, together with his copy of *Treasure Island*.

He retraced his path to the side door of the main building. Now came the difficult part: the dash across the twenty yards of open space to the car. Suddenly he had a terrible thought: what if the boot were locked? Why didn't I think of that before! he asked himself. He realized it was too late now, he'd just have to take the chance.

Suddenly he was scared. His hands were sweating, his mouth was parched. He remembered he was still not well. But he also remembered Ellen, and his last sight of her in

89

the customs queue; and Dad, being carried out on the stretcher to the ambulance; and, more dimly, Mum, running down the hillside in Wales, her long, dark hair streaming behind her. He stood still, counted slowly to ten, and then sprinted to the car.

It seemed like minutes rather than seconds before he reached it. He crouched down behind the boot. The silver lever was exactly at eye level. He grabbed it: it turned, and clicked open. He pushed his case into one corner, clambered in, and drew the boot down again, holding on to a bar inside the flap. Then he found he couldn't close it properly. The sweat was pouring from him: someone's bound to notice, he thought. He tried frantically to pull it shut, then realized it could only be done from the outside. He tried to get more comfortable, using his case as a pillow.

Then he heard footsteps. Lunch must already be over, he thought. The footsteps stopped. Joe realized there were no voices, only a sudden silence. He felt his skin go cold. What happened next was frightening, and puzzling. At one side of the boot flap there was a scrabbling noise, something was dropped through the gap, a gruff voice whispered 'Good luck, mate!' and the footsteps went away.

Joe held his breath. There was silence once more. Very, very slowly he moved his body, and felt around for the object that had been dropped into the boot. Then he found it: a bulky envelope. In this narrow space it was hard to open. Joe got a surprise: inside were two bars of chocolate. Then he realized whose voice it was—Old Wal's! Of course, he thought, he never has lunch with the rest, he always brings his own sandwiches. He must have been looking out of his window and seen what I was doing.

Joe grinned, and whispered: 'Thanks, Wal.'

The heat settled around him. At last he heard several voices, including Mr Piggot's.

'We'll see you in the spring, Mr Jenkins,' he heard him say.

An unfamiliar, English voice replied: 'Yes, indeed. And thanks very much for the lunch.'

Joe heard the door being opened. He felt the car shake as its driver climbed in. The door slammed, the engine started, and the car began to move, at first slowly, then with increasing speed along the bumpy road.

Joe held the fingers of both hands crossed as tightly as he possibly could, and tried to imagine he was back in London, getting a lift through the park in Dad's car .

Chapter 8

DOMESTIC SERVICE

Ellen remained glued to the window, absorbed by the changing shapes and colours of the land far beneath her. So this is what Australia is *really* like, she thought. All those maps we had to draw in geography, all those towns and rivers we had to learn: here they are right below me!

The little plane had been flying for several hours. Sometimes she had seen nothing but rock and mountains, tinted orange by the sun, interrupted by wide, deep-blue rivers curling across the land. At other times they had passed over huge stretches of green, dotted with swamps and creeks like tiny puddles on a lawn. Occasionally, Ellen would catch sight of a town far below, often with little more than half a dozen rooftops. After those weeks trapped inside the orphanage, she could hardly believe what she was seeing.

These sights made her forget for a while why she was on the plane at all, and the fact that every minute she was going further and further away from Joe. Then she remembered the events of the day before.

She had imagined she and Lizzie would be moved to another orphanage, but this time one that wasn't Catholic. As soon as they were in the car and driving away from the orphanage, Ellen had asked Miss Reed about Joe. She had told her he was safe and happy at a farm school, and that she would let her have the address so she could write to him.

'But first let's deal with your future,' she said briskly. 'You girls have caused us a great deal of inconvenience because of what has happened. At the moment we don't have a single spare place in any of our other institutions.'

'Where will we be going then?' Ellen asked anxiously.

'Luckily we have a few families who are prepared to offer girls from England a kind of foster home for a while, in exchange for some domestic service. The idea is that you stay with them, help a bit around the house to pay for your board, and attend the local school. But I must stress that, after what has just happened, you will both be on trial there: we shall be looking for much more responsible behaviour.'

'That sounds all right,' said Lizzie quickly, squeezing Ellen's hand. 'Where is this place?'

'Yours is a couple of hours east from here,' Miss Reed replied. 'We should be there by lunch time. The other house is further away.'

Ellen and Lizzie looked at each other in horror.

'But won't we be in the same house?' Lizzie burst out.

'That's quite impossible. These people have little enough room as it is.'

'But we could share a room, couldn't we?' Ellen said.

'The arrangements are made now. In any case, it seems to me wiser to separate the two of you in the light of recent events. You will, of course, be able to write to each other.'

Neither Ellen nor Lizzie was able to speak for the rest of the journey. Ellen was shocked. In a very short time she had become great friends with Lizzie. She knew it was Lizzie who had kept them going in their battle with the Sisters. Without her courage they would both still be back in the orphanage, miserable and defeated. She glanced at Lizzie from time to time, and saw she was also upset. She wished they could talk, but it was impossible with Miss Reed there.

Finally they turned off the long, unending main road and came into a small town. Miss Reed stopped the car outside a large, white, wooden house set back from the street, and turned to the two girls. 'It's round the back. Just wait there a moment, I'll make sure they're in. You can get your cases out, Lizzie.'

Lizzie took her two cases out of the boot. Ellen got out

too, and stood uncertainly on the hot road. 'It looks like quite a nice place,' she said miserably.

Lizzie looked around. 'It can't be worse than the orphanage, I suppose.' Then she glanced at Ellen. 'I wonder where you'll be? Do you suppose we'll be able to see each other?'

'I don't know.'

Just then Miss Reed called and waved to Lizzie to come over. She picked up her cases, and gave Ellen a quick, sad smile.

''Bye then,' she said, and walked away.

''Bye,' Ellen called. She climbed back into the car, feeling horribly alone.

They drove on to the next town. As they went, Miss Reed explained to Ellen that she would be going from there to a small town two hundred miles away. They had arranged for her to get a ride on the local mail plane, which took that route every week to deliver and pick up people's letters and parcels.

Ellen had never flown in an aeroplane. Planes to her meant wartime fighters and bombers, and anxious moments scanning the sky. But when they reached the small airstrip and she saw the small red and white plane, she felt suddenly excited.

There were three other passengers, two young men and an older woman, as well as several crates of fruit stowed in the back alongside the grey mailbags. Ellen was allowed to sit behind the pilot, who was dressed in just a pair of shorts.

'OK, young lady, it'll be a bit bumpy at first, but you'll soon get the hang of it,' he said cheerily. 'Here we go then.'

The engine started up, and soon they were speeding down the airstrip, and into the air. Ellen looked down through the window, and saw a group of cattle break into a run as the shadow of the plane passed over them. She smiled. Looking back, she saw Miss Reed standing on the airstrip, becoming smaller and smaller as the plane pulled away from the sun-bleached land. Only then did she realize she had forgotten to get addresses for Joe and Lizzie from her.

The plane stopped four times before it reached Ellen's town. At each stop she and the other passengers got out, while the mail was taken out and put into a car or truck by the man collecting it. He and the pilot would have a drink or a smoke before they took off again.

There were usually several people waiting at each airstrip. Ellen realized they had simply come to watch the plane land and take off again. Often there were children there; and at one stop she noticed a family of black-skinned people, standing slightly apart. At once she remembered her geography lesson: these must be the Aboriginals, who came here hundreds of years before Captain Cook arrived. Although there had been two Indian girls in her school in London, she had never seen anyone this dark before. She found it hard not to stare at them.

Eventually, they reached her town. She was glad to see it was bigger than the places they had stopped at before. As the plane came in to land, she wondered which of the houses below would be hers. Suddenly all the excitement of the journey vanished, as she realized she was a complete stranger here.

The usual small crowd was waiting on the airstrip, screening their eyes against the late afternoon sun. As Ellen got down from the plane and said goodbye to the pilot, a small man with a wrinkled face called out from a nearby truck.

'You the English girl for the Lewis's house?' he asked gruffly.

'Yes, I am,' Ellen replied.

'You can put your bags in the back,' he said.

She did so, and climbed into the seat alongside him. There was a strong smell of sweat inside the truck.

'Is it far?' Ellen asked.

'Far enough,' the man grumbled, and spat out of the window. Ellen wondered if the man lived in the Lewis's house. She was relieved when he stopped the truck and said: 'This is where I drop you. It's the end house.'

Ellen walked across a patch of dry grass, and knocked at the door, which swung slowly open under the pressure of her knuckles. She knocked again, waited, then went in. A door to her right was open, and she found herself in a kitchen, standing opposite a small girl with dark curly hair eating at the table.

'Who are you?' the girl said, her mouth half full.

'I'm Ellen. And who are *you*?'

'I'm Grace and I'm six,' the girl said. 'That's Charlie, but he's only a dirty little baby.'

Ellen saw a baby sitting on the sofa, chewing on some object, and pointing at her.

'Is this the right house for Mrs Lewis?' she asked the girl.

'That's my mum.'

'Is your mum at home?'

'She's feeding the hens. We've only got three, 'cos Sally died.'

Ellen couldn't help smiling. 'Oh dear, that's a shame.'

'No, it isn't. She was a stupid hen. She never laid any eggs.'

Just then the back door opened. A large, red-haired woman came in, carrying an empty bowl. Her face was pale, almost white, with dark rings under her eyes, and a small scar above one eyebrow. Seeing Ellen, she frowned.

'Let yourself in, I see,' she said, moving across to the sink.

'I . . . did knock, but there was no answer,' Ellen said nervously.

'There wouldn't be, would there: I can't be in two places at once,' the woman replied, as she rinsed out the bowl.

'I'm sorry,' Ellen said, feeling uncomfortable.

'I want some more bread, Mum: I'm still hungry,' Grace said, in a whining voice.

'God, what's the little blighter up to now?' Mrs Lewis said, ignoring her daughter, and rushing over to the baby. She pulled a piece of wood out of his mouth. 'No, you're not to eat that! Dirty!' She gave him a smack on the hand, and the baby started crying loudly.

'Mum, I'm hungry!' Grace wailed.

'You deserve to be,' her mother replied. 'I told you to watch what he was doing. I can never rely on you, can I?'

Ellen spoke up. 'I'm sorry, I think it was my fault; I was talking to her.'

Mrs Lewis looked coldly at Ellen. 'You'd better make yourself useful then, hadn't you? I've got the supper to prepare. You can keep the kids quiet; make sure they finish their tea.'

'What about my cases?'

'They're not going to walk off by themselves, are they?'

She put the baby, still whimpering, in a high chair. Ellen sat next to him, and kept an eye on the children eating. At the same time she watched Mrs Lewis as she moved around the kitchen, muttering to herself, and banging cupboard doors and saucepans. Ellen felt uneasy with this bad-tempered woman, who never looked you in the eye. Will she always be as nasty as this? she wondered anxiously.

When tea was finished, Mrs Lewis wiped her hands on her dress, and picked up Charlie.

'All right, I'll show you where you're sleeping,' she said to Ellen. To her surprise, Mrs Lewis walked out into the garden. Ellen followed her, past the chicken run and the broken fence, to a wooden shed at the end of the small garden. She opened the door.

'You've got all you need here. Supper will be in half an hour.'

Ellen looked around. The hut was small and shabby, with a bare wooden floor and walls. Apart from the bed, there was just a chair, a chest of drawers with some of its handles broken, and a small shelf above the bed, with an empty silver picture frame on it.

Ellen slowly unpacked. She took out the photograph of Mum, Dad, Joe and herself, sitting on a hillside in Wales. She remembered the merry face of the man who had agreed to take their picture, and the high wind that kept blowing Dad's hat off, and how Mum and Joe had chased after it, and the crisp, green apple she had eaten just before the photo was taken. Ellen sighed, and propped the picture up against the frame. She sat on the bed, remembering other details of that happy day. Then, in the fading light, she walked back to the house.

In the kitchen the table was laid. Mrs Lewis was sitting reading a magazine. 'He's not back yet, we'll have to wait,' she said, glancing up at Ellen. They sat there in silence. Ellen felt more and more awkward.

'What does Mr Lewis do?' she said eventually.

'At this time of night, he drinks,' Mrs Lewis said, looking up at the clock. 'I'll give him ten more minutes.'

They were half-way through the meal when Mr Lewis arrived. Ellen was surprised. For some reason, she had imagined him to be a large man with a black beard. Instead, he was fair-haired, clean-shaven and small. He seemed nervous, and spoke in a high-pitched voice.

'Ah, the girl from England,' he said. 'Yes, well, finding your way around all right, are you?'

'Yes, thank you,' Ellen replied.

'Good, good.' He looked anxiously at his wife as she brought his meal out of the oven. 'The kids asleep, are they?'

'What do you expect at this hour?'

'Ah yes. I got talking a bit . . .'

'Don't waste your breath,' she interrupted, and put his plate of stew in front of him. Mr Lewis glanced nervously at Ellen, and began to eat.

Little was said during the meal. Mrs Lewis read a magazine, while her husband asked Ellen one or two more questions, each time looking at his wife before he did so. After a while he fell silent, and Ellen did the same. She wondered if there were going to be quarrels like this every night. She felt cast down at the thought, and waited miserably for the meal to end so that she could escape to her hut in the garden, where at least she could be alone.

During the next few days, Ellen wondered if she might have been better off in the orphanage. At least there were other girls there: here there was nobody of her age, and nothing to do but work and work and work.

Mrs Lewis made it clear she would be expected to look after Grace a good deal of the time—especially when she had to go and visit her mother at the other side of the town. This she did almost every day, so Ellen quickly got used to feeding and washing Grace, telling her stories, and playing games with her in the garden.

Fortunately, Grace was a lively girl, and often fun to be with. But for the rest of the time Ellen did nothing but housework—dusting, cleaning, scrubbing floors, washing clothes—or going to the shops. Although she had often helped out at home, it was different when Mum or Dad asked you to do something. There you *wanted* to help, but you could be let off if you had a good excuse. There was none of that with Mrs Lewis. Every day she would simply tell Ellen what needed doing, give her the money for shopping, and leave her to it. Ellen realized that she had no choice but to do as she was told.

She saw little of Mr Lewis, who went off early each morning to work in the town, and came back late in the evenings, often missing supper altogether. He and his wife said little to each other, except when they had an argument, which was quite often, especially late at night. Ellen would lie in her hut, and hear their voices getting louder and louder. Then a door would slam, and all would be quiet.

She hated the hours of housework, especially in the middle of the day, when the heat made work difficult, and flies would settle everywhere. She was glad when she could break off to go to the stores. Sometimes, if Mrs Lewis was at home, she would be able to go by herself rather than take Grace with her. She found it difficult at first trying to learn how much food cost. But the store assistants were helpful enough.

She had arrived during the school holidays. Soon she began to wonder when the new term would start. One evening she asked Mrs Lewis, but she just muttered 'School, huh!' Ellen realized she would have to find out some other way. The next time she was in town, she asked one of the store assistants where the school was. A few minutes later she was standing outside a group of low iron buildings in one of the side streets.

'Looking for someone?' A dark-haired young woman was leaning out of one of the windows, paint brush in hand. Ellen walked over to her.

'Excuse me, is this the school?' she said.

'Yes—at least it usually is,' the woman replied. 'At the moment there are more pots of paint here than children.' She smiled, and Ellen smiled back, liking the woman's pretty, mischievous face. 'I'm just finishing off in here,' she continued. 'Come through, the door's open.'

Ellen went inside, walked through a corridor, and found the classroom. It was light and warm, and smelt of new paint. The woman was kneeling, painting the wall beneath the windowsill.

'Have a seat, I won't be a second. I'm Miss Carvel, I teach here at the school—or at least I try to. What's your name?'

'Ellen Duffy.'

Miss Carvel turned and gave Ellen a look. 'You're English, by the sound of it.'

'Yes.'

'I went to England once. Just before the war. It's a fascinating country. Which part are you from?'

'From London; I live in Battersea.'

'Oh yes, I remember seeing the name on a bus—I went to London a couple of times. But I was in Yorkshire mostly. It was beautiful there, the countryside.'

She turned back, painted a few more strokes with the brush, then put it down and stood up. 'Are you just passing through?'

'I'm staying with Mr and Mrs Lewis.'

'I don't think I know them. Enjoying it?'

Ellen was silent. She was more cautious with adults now. How do I know I can trust her, she thought? 'I've not been there long,' she said finally.

Miss Carvel stood back to look at what she had done. Ellen noticed that she was slim and tall. 'That's a bit more cheerful. What do you think of my choice then, Ellen?'

'I like it.'

'Good. Let's hope the other children have taste like you.' She sat on one of the desks near the window. 'So, what brings you to our little town?'

Ellen hesitated. She liked Miss Carvel's warm blue eyes and the way she treated her as if she were grown up. She felt she could trust her, and suddenly found herself telling her all about the events of the last few months.

Miss Carvel listened sympathetically, her cheerful face now serious, now sad, as Ellen told her story. 'You poor girl, you *have* had a dreadful time, haven't you?' she said eventually. 'And fancy ending up in a place like this! I was a stranger here not so long ago: I used to teach in the city. So I know just how you feel. And how do you spend your time here?'

'I have to work most of the time for Mrs Lewis. That's why I came here, to find out when school starts.'

'You'd like to join us, would you?'

'Oh, yes,' said Ellen, seeing the chance of spending time away from the Lewis's house.

'How long are you here for?'

'A few months, I think.'

'In that case it's a good idea, and I'm sure we can

101

organize it. There'll certainly be room for you in the older class—that's my group. You'll find it a bit different from your school in England, though.'

'I don't mind,' Ellen said quickly. 'I'm quite good at subjects like history and geography.'

Miss Carvel studied her for a moment, looked at her watch, and stood up. 'Tell you what, Ellen. I have to go now, I'm late already. Give me the address where you're staying, and I'll drop by later in the week. I'll tell you what we did last term, and we'll see what you feel then about coming here.'

'Oh, thank you,' Ellen said. As she walked out of the school with Miss Carvel, she forgot her unhappiness for a moment. It felt wonderful to talk like this with a grown-up who didn't tell you off, and who seemed to want to help. Suddenly she felt less trapped.

The next few days seemed to go very slowly. If she had to go to town, Ellen tried to do the shopping in double quick time, in case Miss Carvel turned up while she was out. She was also worried that Mrs Lewis might be in when she called, because then it would be more difficult to stop work.

As it was, there seemed to be more things than ever to do about the house. But Ellen was puzzled: she couldn't understand why everything had to be kept so spotlessly clean, when hardly anyone came to visit. Apart from one neighbour, whose child Grace sometimes went to play with, no one else had been inside the door since Ellen came.

When Miss Carvel did come, Ellen was on her knees scrubbing the porch. She got up quickly, and tried unsuccessfully to hide the bucket of water and cloth, ashamed of what she was doing.

'Hello, Ellen: have I chosen a bad moment?' Miss Carvel said.

Ellen blushed. 'No, that's all right, I've almost finished,' she said, aware of Miss Carvel's pretty blue dress and fresh freckled face, compared to her own shabby overalls and sweating forehead.

'Well, if you're sure. Shall we sit here, or would you rather be inside in the cool?'

Ellen hesitated. 'Mrs Lewis isn't here. We could sit in the kitchen.'

She brought Miss Carvel through to the kitchen, poured her some iced water, and found some biscuits. For a moment it was as if this was *her* home. Then, saying she had to wash her hands, she went to her hut, and changed into her favourite green skirt and white cotton top.

'How nice you look,' Miss Carvel said, when she returned. 'This is a real party we're having.'

She held up her glass in celebration, and Ellen, feeling at ease now, did the same.

'Now, Ellen,' Miss Carvel began, 'I thought first I'd see where you were with maths and English. If you'd like to just answer the questions on these two sheets, then we can talk about the rest. Is that OK?'

'We hardly did school in the orphanage,' Ellen said, anxiously.

'Don't worry, they're not tests, just something that will help me to know what kind of things you've already covered. Look, if you like I'll go into the garden while you fill them in.'

To Ellen's relief, she could recognize and tick all the things that were listed on the two sheets, so she was soon able to call Miss Carvel in.

'Good, that's excellent,' she said, looking down the sheets. 'You obviously won't have any trouble fitting in. In fact, you'll be quite a lot further on than the other children. I'll have to work hard to stop you falling asleep!'

'I won't do that,' Ellen said hurriedly, pleased that she wouldn't be left behind. Miss Carvel laughed, in a way that stirred something in Ellen's memory.

'I'm sure you won't. Now, you said you liked history and geography. Have you done much about Australia?'

'We did a bit—about the different towns and rivers, and the rainfall and—oh yes, all the different animals and birds.'

'That's all useful. Anything on Australian history?'

'No, we only did the history of England.'

'Ah, then you've got a treat coming. Australian history has some wonderful stories. You can hear all about the expeditions into the outback, about the explorers. We're also doing some Aboriginal history.'

'Oh yes, our teacher talked about them. They were here before anyone else, weren't they?'

'Yes, long, long before—perhaps thirty thousand years ago.'

'I think I saw a few of them on the way here, at one of the towns where the plane stopped.'

'Yes, that's very likely. There's a few families here too, they have a camp outside town. I go down there sometimes; I teach some of the men English. It's a bit of a struggle, to be honest.' She laughed again, and Ellen recognized what had tugged at her memory—that was how Mum laughed, it was almost the same light sound.

Just then Mrs Lewis came back. She was carrying Charlie, while Grace came in sulkily just behind her. She stopped when she saw Miss Carvel.

'Who are you?' she said.

'I'm Julie Carvel, I teach at the school.'

'Oh yes?' Mrs Lewis said, looking sharply at Ellen.

'I've just been talking to Ellen about her coming to classes,' Miss Carvel continued. 'I don't think she'll have any problem fitting in.'

Mrs Lewis scowled, and put Charlie down on the sofa. 'Who said anything about school?'

Miss Carvel caught Ellen's eye. 'I gather Ellen was hoping to continue her education while she was here,' she said. 'I'm quite prepared to have her in my class.'

'That's neither here nor there,' Mrs Lewis muttered, looking angrily at Ellen.

'But Miss Reed said I could!' she said fiercely.

'It's not up to her, is it?' Mrs Lewis replied. 'Now, if you'll excuse us, the children need their tea.'

Miss Carvel gathered up her papers. 'I do hope you'll let Ellen come to school, Mrs Lewis,' she said. Mrs Lewis made no reply as they left the room.

'Don't worry, we'll work something out,' Miss Carvel said to Ellen, at the front door. She drew a book out of her bag. 'I've brought this from our little library at school. Bring it back whenever you want to.' She held Ellen's arm for a moment, and smiled once more. ''Bye now, Ellen. I'll see you soon.'

As Ellen watched the small blue car move off, she wondered if she *would* see her soon—or even ever again? Miss Carvel's kindness had raised her spirits. But now it looked as if it would be harder than ever to get away from this miserable house.

Chapter 9

A TASTE OF FREEDOM

The hours in the boot of Mr Jenkins' car were the most uncomfortable Joe could remember. The car jogged up and down the whole time. The boot crashed noisily at every bump in the road. Joe was sure Mr Jenkins would hear it. Worst of all was the dust, which blew up into his face. He was forced to keep his eyes closed, or shift around into an even more uncomfortable position facing away from the road.

The car stopped once for a few minutes. Joe listened carefully to the voices, and realized they were at a garage or petrol station. He decided this was the moment to eat one of his precious bars of chocolate. He wished he had something to drink: his mouth felt completely dry, and his eyes filled with grit.

Once the car started again, he began to feel drowsy. I mustn't go to sleep, he told himself, I must stay awake . . . mustn't sleep, must stay awake . . . sleep, awake . . . sleep, awake . . . Suddenly he was awake once more. The noise had gone, the air felt cooler, and he realized the car had stopped.

He wondered how long he had been asleep, and how long they had been here—perhaps a minute, perhaps an hour. Should I get out now? he thought. He had lost all idea of time. He wondered where they were: he heard the occasional car pass nearby. He decided that if the car didn't start again soon then Mr Jenkins had probably arrived at his home.

After a few minutes Joe took a deep breath, scrambled out of the boot, pulled his suitcase out, closed the flap gently, and looked around. The car was parked at the back of a low wooden building. Next to it, Joe saw other buildings stretching out in a row—they looked like people's homes. In the other direction there was a large patch of wasteland, and then a larger flat building, with a grey tin roof. It looked deserted. Beyond the building was a sight now familiar to Joe: miles and miles of dark pink open land, broken up here and there by blue or green bushes, and patches of white, thistly-looking flowers.

It was still light—probably early evening, Joe thought. He walked quickly over to the deserted building. He looked through a broken window, and then went in. The whole building was just one room, with rows of wooden columns every few feet. At waist level it was divided into sections by small wooden fences, with little openings every few yards. At first Joe thought it was a deserted church. Then he decided it was probably a stable. As he walked slowly down the middle, he noticed black numbers painted on to the wooden beams above him. At one point someone had carved a message into the wood: 'Trevor Harris 307, Roy Clifford 318.'

Joe walked through one of the openings, and sat down on the floor, with his back against the wall. He was suddenly hungry. He got out the other bar of chocolate, and ate it eagerly, wishing again that he had a drink. Then he set his mind to work out what he should do next.

By now they'll have found out I'm missing at the farm, he thought. But they probably won't guess how I escaped—which means that Mr Jenkins won't know where I come from. But how can I ask him about Ellen without him getting suspicious, and wanting to know who I am? Then he had an idea: supposing I tell him the whole story, tell him about what happened to Ken and John, what really goes on at the farm school? Unable to make up his mind what was best, he decided to go round into the street, and see if he could see which house Mr Jenkins was in.

Just then he heard a rustling noise. It was coming from

only a few yards away—there was something there! Joe lay down, keeping as still as he could. What sort of animal was it? Then he heard a loud yawn, and the sound of someone stretching, and above the wooden partition appeared the head of a man. He rolled his head round slowly, then stopped as he saw Joe.

'Strike a light!—who's this sleeping in my hotel?' He looked at Joe in the fading light. 'A nipper! Bit young for a swaggie, aren't you?'

Joe got to his feet, unsure what he meant. The man looked a bit like a tramp, with his messy hair, heavy beard, and dirty, torn shirt. He stretched again.

''Strewth, I needed that bit of sleep. You been here long?'

'No, not very long,' Joe said, relieved that the man seemed friendly.

'Where are you bound for?'

'I'm not sure,' Joe replied, feeling a bit silly. 'I haven't decided yet,' he added.

'Hey, you from New Zealand or something? A bit out of your way, aren't you?'

'No, I'm from England.'

'England! Jesus, that's quite a ride away. And what are you doing here, out in the back of beyond?'

'I've got a few days off from school,' Joe replied, blushing.

He saw the man smile slightly. 'OK, mate, I'm with you. Just having a look round our big, empty country. Feel free—and no more questions. You had any tucker recently?'

'Not much,' Joe said, his stomach rumbling at the thought.

'Here, come over to my room, and we'll get stuck into my tucker bag.'

Joe came round the partition. The man had a sleeping-bag laid out on the floor, and a few possessions strewn around it. He rummaged around in a battered little brown bag, and produced some bread and corned beef. Joe eagerly accepted a piece of each, as well as a swig from the man's water bottle.

They ate without speaking. Then Joe said: 'What is this place?'

'This? It's an old sheep shed,' the man replied. 'Good a place as any to lay your head down. Besides, I feel I'm owed a few nights' rest, after what the bastards did to my dad.'

'What do you mean?' Joe said, feeling easier now he had some food inside him.

'You ever seen a shearer in action? It's a bastard of a job, I can tell you. My dad was one: he'd travel hundreds of miles to get work. On foot most of the time. One of the best, he was, a real ringer. But if the overseer didn't like your face, you didn't get a pen, you ended up sweeping the shed floor—or moving on to find the next run. Yair, it was hard. It killed him in the end.'

'Is that your job as well?' Joe asked.

'Not on your sweet life. I like to keep moving, not be tied to any one man. Why should I bust my guts for someone else? I muster cattle now and then, when I need some money. But then I'm on the move again, hitching a ride or jumping the rattlers. It's a great life.'

'Don't you have your own home, then?'

'Yair, 'course I do—under the stars! They make a beaut of a ceiling. You should try a spot of moonbathing one night.' He looked out of the window. 'Why don't you give it a go tonight, eh?'

This reminded Joe that he still hadn't found out where Mr Jenkins lived. 'I've got to go and meet someone in one of those houses,' he said, standing up. 'He might give me a ride in his car.'

'Sure, time to move on,' the man said, looking at Joe's suitcase. 'Good travelling, mate.'

Joe felt sorry to leave: he'd never met anyone like this man before. He'd like to have heard more about his life. But could it really be so wonderful, travelling around all the time, not having anywhere to come home to? The man seemed to be happy with it; but Joe knew it wouldn't suit him. He thanked him for the food, shook his hand, and walked back through the shed, trying to imagine what it would have been like full of sheep and men.

He walked back across the wasteland, glad that it was almost dark, and that nobody seemed to be about. Then, as he turned into the street, he saw two men talking in front of one of the houses, and recognized the one with his back to him as Mr Jenkins. Joe noticed he had his briefcase with him, which meant that he must be going out to work—perhaps to inspect Ellen's convent school?

Joe walked quickly back the way he had come. As soon as he was out of sight of Mr Jenkins, he made a run for the car. He dashed round to the back, grabbed the boot handle, turned it—and found it was stuck! Desperately he looked towards the houses, then inside the car. Through the window he saw a jumble of boxes and clothes on the back seat. He tried the door handle, and in a few seconds was down on the floor hidden from sight, aware only of the smell of leather, and the sound of his heart throbbing, as if it were the car engine itself.

'. . . He'll get by without his rabbit pie;
So run, rabbit, run, rabbit, run, run, run.'

Mr Jenkins seemed in a good mood. As the car rattled along, he kept breaking into song, and chuckling to himself now and then. All Joe could see was his hand on the gears, the pale fingers drumming in time with the songs. He had a strange, crackly voice, which nearly made Joe laugh out loud.

It was hard for him to keep still, the thought of possibly seeing Ellen again was so exciting. It was strange, Joe thought, when you'd been with someone every day of your life, suddenly not to know where they were, or what they were doing. He hoped her school was nothing like his place, and then remembered that it couldn't be; it was run by nuns, and they were bound to be kind and understanding.

110

After a while Joe noticed the light was fading. Soon the beams from car headlights moved across the inside of the car roof. Feeling stiff from being in one position, he turned slowly on to his side, and saw a box of apples on the floor by his feet. His mouth began to water. He wondered if he could reach one without Mr Jenkins seeing him. Suddenly the car swerved, bumped up and down violently, and stopped abruptly.

'Wretched animal!' muttered Mr Jenkins.

'Oww!' yelled Joe, as the side of his head hit the back of the seat in front.

Mr Jenkins looked round. As his eyes met Joe's, his mouth slowly fell open. 'Good heavens!' he said. 'Who . . . what . . . how did *you* get there?'

Joe held his head and groaned again.

'Are you hurt?'

Joe nodded. Mr Jenkins got out, opened the door nearest to Joe, and looked hard at him.

'Sit up on the seat,' he said. 'That's it. Now, let me look; it's your cheek, is it? Ah yes, there is some blood. But I don't think it's serious.' He took a handkerchief from his pocket. 'Here, hold this against it for the moment.'

Joe did so. Mr Jenkins watched him curiously. 'All right? I think it's more shock than anything else.'

The cut only hurt a bit. But Joe realized that if he pretended to be more shocked than he felt, he wouldn't have to speak for a while, and by then they might have arrived at the school. He leaned his head gently against the side of the car.

'That's a good idea, just take it easy for a bit,' Mr Jenkins said, as if he had read Joe's mind. 'I don't know who you are, but there'll be time for all that later. I'm due to make a call a few miles from here, so just you sit tight, and we'll get some plaster organized. All right?'

Joe nodded, and Mr Jenkins got back into the driver's seat. 'We'll be there in half an hour,' he said. 'Just keep the handkerchief held tight.'

Soon the car turned down into the blackness of a side road, broken only by the two narrow beams of the headlights catching the trees on either side. Joe had worked out his plan. If it *was* Ellen's school they were coming to, then it would be all right: he could tell her everything, and she would know what to do. If it was another school, then he would ask if he could stay there. And if the teachers said no, then he would tell Mr Jenkins everything about the farm school.

The trees came to an end, and the car slowed down as they reached the lighted buildings.—And then Joe stared out in horror. Was he dreaming? No, he couldn't be. They were back at the farm school!

'Here we are at last,' said Mr Jenkins. 'Now if you just wait a mo—hey! Where are you going?'

Joe leapt out of the car and dashed off into the darkness. He had no thought of where he was going—just away, away from that terrible place. He ran and ran, stumbled suddenly, just kept his balance, stumbled again and fell, picked himself up, and ran on blindly. 'Ellen! Ellen!' he shouted into the hot night air. Leaves scratched against his face, he could feel his knee beginning to hurt, but still he ran on. At last, exhausted, he dropped to the ground, and broke into sobs.

He cried for several minutes, until he could do so no more. Then he sat up, touched his cheek, and felt the dry blood on it. Underneath him the grass felt cool and firm. He heard voices, and looking up saw several tiny beams of light zigzagging the sky and the ground not far away. They were getting closer to him, but he had no strength left to move.

'Here he is,' called a voice. Joe shaded his eyes as the arrows of light struck his face.

'Don't worry, no one's going to hurt you, boy,' said another. 'Get up now, we'll take you to the house.'

He stood up, shakily, and felt a hand take him firmly by the arm. Then the torches were shone on the ground, and they moved off. They walked in silence until the house came into view. Then the man holding him bent down and whispered fiercely in his ear: 'No scenes in front of Mr Jenkins now, or you'll get what for!'

By the light of the porch Joe could make out three figures standing there. As Joe and the men came closer, Mr Jenkins stepped forward.

'Is he OK? I thought I'd just hang on for a while, to make sure. I think the knock must have been worse than I realized.'

'He'll be all right, he's just worn out,' said the man holding his arm. 'Probably hasn't slept much in the last twenty-four hours.'

Then, from behind Mr Jenkins, Mr Piggot stepped into the light. Joe began to tremble. He was back in his dream . . . the stick raised up high . . . the cries echoing round the shower room . . . the need to escape. He jerked his arm free, and staggered towards Mr Jenkins.

'Don't let me—' he began. Then the light seemed to go out, and he felt himself falling.

The boys were getting ready for bed when Joe returned to the barn a week later. Immediately several boys crowded round him.

'We thought you'd done it, Joe.'

'You should have seen Old Pig Face!'

'Boy, was he annoyed!'

'They looked *everywhere* for you.'

'And guess what, we didn't have to do any work that afternoon.'

'Yes, they were all out on search parties.'

Joe grinned, and looked at Andy. 'And they didn't guess how I escaped?'

'No,' Andy said. 'Old Wal says they thought you'd gone out into the bush, like Jamie.'

Joe opened his mouth to tell them how Wal had seen him get into the boot. But then he stopped himself. I don't want to get him into trouble, he thought. Instead he told them the details of his journey. Then he remembered something that had been puzzling him ever since he got back.

'But why did Mr Jenkins come all the way back here?' Joe asked Andy. 'Did Wal say anything about that?'

'Yes,' Andy replied. 'He left his present behind. Wal says Piggot always gives him something, so that he'll write them a good report. So he came back for it.'

'What did he get?'

'Wal didn't know—he says it must have been something pretty good, for him to drive all this way to fetch it.'

Joe was reminded again of the shock he felt at finding himself back at the farm, and how he had passed out in front of Mr Jenkins. He remembered coming round, and seeing faces, and being lifted and carried up some stairs. But it was only when he awoke much, much later, and found himself in the sick bed again, with daylight showing through the curtains, that he finally realized his attempt to escape had failed, and that Ellen remained as far away as ever. And now he knew that, even if he *had* been able to speak to Mr Jenkins, it probably wouldn't have made any difference. He's on Piggot's side really, he wouldn't have wanted to help. There's no way out after all, he thought miserably.

For a while, because of his adventure, Joe was the centre of attention. He was no longer simply one of the younger new boys, with just a few friends his own age. He was aware of being looked at and noticed by others quite a bit older. That made him feel pleased and important. Several boys talked to him for the first time. He was especially pleased when Ken came over during one of the breaks from work, punched him playfully on the arm, and said: 'Good try, kid: we'll beat 'em yet.'

On the other hand, Joe soon realized that the staff also took more interest in him—but for very different reasons. On the first day back on the building site, Mr Temple took him aside.

'OK, Duffy lad, you've had your bit of fun—and wasted a lot of our time into the bargain. So we'll have to keep a special eye on you, won't we? Make sure you're nice and busy all the time, eh? For a start, you can clean out the lavatories by the barn.'

'But boys don't have to do that,' Joe said.

'Some boys do,' Mr Temple replied, smiling grimly. 'I should get used to the idea pretty damn quick if I were you.'

From that day on, Joe was picked on for the dirtiest, most unpleasant jobs around the farm. He was also given a lot of extra work: clearing up the building site at the end of the day, washing the cement and dirt off the tools, helping the cook wash up. There had never been much time to rest or play, but now there was even less. Often he went to bed exhausted, wondering how he was going to get up in the morning.

It was quite a while before he was able to visit Old Wal. He wanted to thank him for the bars of chocolate. Finally, on an afternoon when Mr Temple had gone off to get building materials from the nearby town, he found some time to spare. He was relieved to find Wal on his own.

'Ah, Joe, I hoped I wouldn't be seeing you again,' Wal said, looking up from his account book, and grinning.

'So did I,' said Joe.

'You had bad luck, mate. Who would have guessed it?'

'I came to say thanks for the bars of chocolate.'

'The pleasure's mine, sport,' he said.

Joe became thoughtful. 'Wal, why is everyone so nasty to us here?' he said. 'It's not fair. We haven't done anything wrong, have we?'

'No, you haven't,' Wal said. 'They shouldn't be allowed, the kind of things that go on here.' There was anger in his voice.

'But why *are* they allowed?' Joe asked.

Wal leant forward, his voice quieter. 'Because nobody knows about them—or if they do, they don't *want* to know.'

'But what about Australian boys; are their schools like this?'

'Oh no. But they're lucky, you see, they have families—or at least most of them do.'

'But so do I.'

'*You* do?' Wal looked in surprise at Joe.

'Yes.'

'What, mother or father?'

'Both. But they're back in England.'

'Then why on earth are you over here?'

Then Joe told Wal all about Mum going off, and Dad's illness, and the time they spent in the Home, and how they had been suddenly sent to Australia without understanding where they were going, and what a shock it had been when he and Ellen had been separated.

Wal listened with a frown, shaking his large head from time to time. 'That's a hard-luck story if ever I heard one,' he said, when Joe finished. 'And you've not had any contact with your family since then?'

'No,' Joe replied. 'I thought of writing a letter, to my Aunty Muriel in Derby, but I don't know her address.'

Wal grunted. 'Huh, I don't think she'd get it anyway, not that sort of letter.'

'Why not?'

'Let's just say they like to keep a close watch on what goes out of this place.'

'What do you mean?'

Wal leaned forward again. 'This is between you and me, OK, Joe? I don't want to get into trouble.' Joe nodded. 'Well, if any of you write a letter home, Piggot reads it

116

first. Any bad stories, and the letter never gets to the mail box.'

Joe gasped. 'But that's unfair, letters are private!'

'Of course they are. But fairness doesn't count for much here!'

Wal stood up and looked out through the window. Joe sighed. That's what I don't understand, he thought. Everything seems to be upside down. Most grown-ups seemed to be on our side before. But ever since that day Mum left home, they've all been against us—except Wal.

'Tell me one thing,' said Wal, turning away from the window, and sitting on the edge of his desk. 'Who's living in your house in London now?'

'I don't know,' Joe said. He realized he had never imagined anyone else living there. How could they be? It was *his* house, his and Ellen's and Mum's and Dad's.

'It might have been rented out to someone. Your aunt could have arranged that, perhaps?'

'I suppose so,' Joe replied, hating the idea, especially if Aunty Muriel had anything to do with it.

'Well, if you wrote to your dad there, telling him you're not happy here, with a bit of luck someone might post it on to his nursing home.'

Joe's eyes opened wide. 'Would they?' he said eagerly. Then he remembered. 'But the letter won't get there, will it?'

'That depends who you give it to.' He opened a drawer inside his desk. 'Here's some paper and a pencil. Go away and write to your dad, and bring the letter back to me before Friday, when I have to go into town. I'll make damn sure it gets posted.'

'Will you really?' Joe said, suddenly hopeful again.

'But don't let anyone see you writing, not even your friends.'

'OK,' Joe said. And he left with a smile on his face.

That evening, while most of the boys were playing football outside the barn, Joe locked himself in one of the cubicles in the nearby lavatories.

It wasn't an easy letter. Joe realized that he'd never written to Dad before—he'd never had to, they'd always been together. Now he felt awkward and uncertain, as though he wasn't quite sure what Dad was like. At first he kept crossing out what he had written, using up several pieces of the pad Wal had given him. Finally he finished, and read it through, to make sure he'd not left out anything important.

Dear Dad,

I hope you are getting better in your nursing home. I didn't like it when you were ill and had to go in the ambulance. When will you be able to do your job again? I hope it is soon.

I am in Australia now, but I'm not very happy, and that's why I am writing this letter. A man called Wal who is very nice is going to post it on Friday, but we don't know who is living at our house now, do you? I don't like the men here, you have to work hard all the time, it's horrible, and the weather is very hot, and if you don't work hard they hit you with sticks, it's not fair.

Also we don't get very much school as we are always working on the new building or cleaning out the places where the animals live, they have pigs here and hens and horses because it's really a farm.

Where is Mum, have you had a letter from her? I forgot to tell you it is only boys here, Ellen is somewhere else but I don't know the name of her school, except it is run by nuns. After we got off the ship I got on the train with the boys and then it started without her.

One day I ran away to try and find her school, because the man who comes to do an inspection had a car just like our one, and I had a ride in the boot for a long time, but then he came back here again and they found me.

We went on a ship to come here and before that we were in a place called Bethesda Home for Children, but that was horrible as well, except we didn't have to work so hard.

I hope you get this letter, and if you are better can we come home now?

Love from Joe.

'How long will it take?' he asked Wal, as soon as he found a moment to bring him the letter.

'That's difficult to say,' Wal replied. 'But I'll send it air mail, so it will go as quickly as possible.'

Joe suddenly had an awful thought. 'I didn't put the address on—Dad won't know where to write back.'

'That doesn't matter,' Wal said. 'I was going to put a note inside, telling your dad a bit about what's going on here. My home address will be on that—and he can write back to me there, so Piggot won't get hold of it.'

'Oh yes, that's a good idea.'

'But remember one thing, Joe.'

'What?'

Wal put a hand on his shoulder. 'It's better not to get too excited about all this. You see, you may not get an answer. The house may have been sold. Do you understand that?'

'Yes,' Joe replied.

But it was too late. In his mind he could already see the letter falling through the narrow letter-box into the hall, and Dad coming downstairs in his green dressing-gown, and opening the letter, and reading it, and then sitting down at the kitchen table to write back to him.

No, the house hadn't been sold, that was impossible.

Chapter 10

THE STRUGGLE

The sun woke her suddenly. Ellen got out of bed. She lifted the mattress, and pulled the book out from underneath it. She drew the curtains back to let more sunlight in, and settled back into bed.

This was the first chance she had had to look at the book Miss Carvel had left the day before. Mrs Lewis seemed to be giving her more work than ever, and she hadn't had a free moment until now. Looking through the book made Ellen want to go to school even more. The idea of doing nothing but work in this hateful house for weeks and weeks filled her with dread.

Now that she had seen different parts of Australia from the air, she was keen to find out about its history. The book had lots of stories about the early years—of convicts and gold diggers in the outback, of daring outlaws and determined explorers. It seemed much more exciting than the book they had used at school. For the next few mornings she found it hard to stop reading when it was time to get up.

Later that week, when Ellen was cleaning the chicken run, Mr Lewis came into the garden and stood watching her. Although he often took his lunch break at home when Mrs Lewis was at her mother's, he had never before come out and spoken to her while she was working.

'Making a fair job of that, I see,' he said eventually.

Ellen stopped, and wiped her brow. 'I hope so,' she said.

'Yes, you seem to be a good little worker. Don't think we haven't noticed that.'

'Thank you,' she said, surprised at the compliment.

He moved down the garden, then walked back towards her. 'What would you say to a little bit of pocket money, eh?'

'Pocket money? What would I have to do?'

'Oh, just carry on pretty much as you are. Nothing new really.'

Ellen plucked up her courage. 'Can I go to school?'

Mr Lewis shuffled his feet, and glanced back at the house. 'I don't think that would be approved of, no.'

'But everyone else goes; why can't I?' she said, feeling a little bolder.

'Ah, well they live here, you see. You're only here for a few months; there's not much point, is there?'

'But that's what's supposed to happen,' Ellen said, feeling her throat tighten. 'It's unfair.'

'You can't always have what you want, you know,' he replied, backing away slightly, as if he was scared of Ellen.

'I don't care what you say, I'm going anyway!' she said fiercely, suddenly aware of her heart beating.

He looked directly at her for the first time. 'I wouldn't do that if I were you,' he said. 'That's not a good idea at all.' And he walked back quickly to the house.

'Look, Ellen! That's the Aboriginals' camp over there.'

Ellen peered through the car window to where Miss Carvel was pointing. Across the flat open land she saw a collection of low buildings, strung out in front of a group of trees. It looked a bare and empty place for a home, she thought.

'Wouldn't they rather live in the town?' she asked, as the car turned towards the buildings.

'Some do. But a lot prefer to be separate, to keep their own way of life. Not that it's been easy for them to do that.'

'Mr Lewis says they're just like children, and that they're always getting drunk.'

121

Miss Carvel frowned. 'That's nonsense, Ellen. But I'm afraid it's what a lot of white people think—especially those who've never talked to them properly. And then they wonder why they're suspicious of white people.'

As the car came towards the camp, Ellen wondered if it had been such a good idea to come. When Mrs Lewis had told her that morning that she was taking the whole family to her sister's for the day, she could hardly believe her luck. That means I can find some time to take the book back and see Miss Carvel again, she had thought. As soon as the house was empty, she had run as fast as she could to the school—and found Miss Carvel about to leave for the Aboriginal camp. Ellen had immediately accepted her invitation to go with her. But now they were here, she felt nervous.

Miss Carvel led her across the hard, dry earth to the buildings. They passed several small huts, made of branches and grass, and open at the sides so that you could see right into them. Ellen was surprised to find many of the men wearing ordinary clothes, and the women in colourful dresses.

They walked past and over to one of the sheds, where three men were waiting. 'That's some of my class,' Miss Carvel said. 'The one in the middle is the elder, the chief man of the group. I'll explain to him who you are.'

Ellen hung back while she spoke to the man. She watched his black serious face, his broad forehead covered in lines, as he listened to Miss Carvel, and then nodded gravely at Ellen. The two younger men looked in her direction: one of them grinned, and she realized she had been staring at them.

'They welcome you,' Miss Carvel said, coming back over. 'They're friendly people, once they feel you respect them. Anyway, Ellen, you're free to watch the lesson, or wander about and explore, whatever you like. See you soon.'

Miss Carvel went and sat on an old box on the verandah, and a small group of men formed round her, sitting themselves on two old bedsteads, or leaning against the corrugated iron wall of the building. Ellen watched and listened, absorbed by the strangeness of hearing familiar English words float across the afternoon air. Although it was hot even in the shade, she felt more comfortable now.

Suddenly three Aboriginal girls came running round the corner of the building, stopping suddenly as they saw Ellen. They were all, she noticed, about her own age, and were wearing long, rather ragged white dresses, which came down almost to their ankles. They stood and stared. Ellen smiled at them, feeling a bit awkward. Then they drifted away, and sat on the ground in front of one of the nearby huts. Another girl brought a basket out from one of the huts, and the four of them crouched on the floor around it.

Now and again they looked towards Ellen. Soon she wandered across to them. They glanced at her, then carried on with their game. She saw they were making shapes in the ground with lots of tiny coloured pebbles, taking turns with a handful each. Squatting down next to them, she could make out a bull, and what looked like a half-finished horse.

The girl next to her took hold of the basket, came over to Ellen, and placed it on the ground in front of her. Ellen understood, took a handful of pebbles, and placed them along the unfinished back leg of the horse. Then she passed the basket on to the next girl.

After that, the girls became less reserved with Ellen. They shared with her some fruit which one of the women had brought out to them. They took her over to the outskirts of the camp, where there was a single slab of dark red rock. They all scrambled nimbly up it, stopping now and then to let Ellen catch up. From the top there was a clear view of the whole plain. Ellen thought again what a lonely country it must be to live in.

123

Afterwards they ran races in the soft dust behind the main building. Ellen took off her shoes and joined in, enjoying the wind on her face, and the chance to let herself go—even though she usually came in last.

Then Miss Carvel appeared from the other side of the building. 'You look like you're having a good time,' she called out.

Ellen came across to her, hot and breathless. She suddenly remembered her work, and her face tightened up. 'I suppose we have to go now?' she said.

'Would you like to stay on for a bit?' Miss Carvel said. 'They're having a corroboree soon—that's their name for a dance.'

'I'd like to,' said Ellen anxiously. 'But Mrs Lewis said she'd be back at ten o'clock. Will there be time?'

Miss Carvel looked at her watch. 'We can probably catch the beginning. Then I'll drive you straight back.'

Soon, as dusk came on and fires were lit, the men emerged from their huts, their bodies covered with paint. Ellen was amazed at all the different patterns of white lines and spots that criss-crossed the men's chests, arms and legs, each one different from the next. She noticed some of the smaller boys had also been painted, but that the girls she had been playing with were still in their white dresses.

'That's the didgeridoo,' Miss Carvel said, as they watched an older man starting to blow through a long piece of wood, holding it between his toes. A strange low sound came out of it. Soon several men were performing a dance, each holding a bunch of feathers in his hand. Ellen saw one of the painted boys edge into the circle, and try to imitate the actions of the men, who were stamping the ground, every now and then producing short, sharp cries to the rhythm of the music.

As the darkness deepened, Ellen began to see only the painted white patterns as the men danced, as if she were watching slow-moving skeletons. The music grew louder. She found herself swaying to its beat, and saw Miss Carvel was doing so too. Their eyes met happily for a moment in the warm firelight. Suddenly Ellen thought to herself, if only Joe was here now.

As the car came within sight of the Lewis's house, Ellen saw to her horror that the lights were on.

'Oh no, they must be back already,' she said.

Miss Carvel stopped the car. 'Will you get into trouble?' she said.

'I don't know,' Ellen replied.

'Don't worry, I'll come in and explain,' Miss Carvel said. 'After all, it was my idea in the first place.'

Ellen rang the bell, but nothing happened. She rang again. Finally they heard footsteps. Mr Lewis opened the door.

'Oh, it's you,' he said. 'I thought for a moment you'd run away.'

His voice was squeakier than ever. Ellen realized he had been drinking again. His head rolled slightly, and he looked suspiciously at Miss Carvel.

'You're that teacher woman, aren't you?' he said.

'Yes, that's right. I'm very sorry about Ellen being late, Mr Lewis. It's my fault, I was going out to the camp, and I just thought she would—'

'The blacks' camp, you mean, out in the arse end of nowhere? Oh yes, you're the Abos' friend, aren't you? I remember.' He swayed slightly, and laughed. 'You want to know the truth about those boongs? They don't have any brains at all, they're just like kids, real dunderheads. Look at the rags they go around in. They're not interested in work, all they want is their grog, so most of the time they're half seas over.'

'I can't agree with you there,' Miss Carvel said firmly.

'I don't give a stuff about what you think, young lady. I know your kind: you read a bloody book or two and you think you know it all.'

'On the contrary—'

'Listen, we're not in school now, so let's not waste time talking about it.' He turned back to Ellen. 'I've been waiting too long for my tucker already.'

'Isn't Mrs Lewis back yet?' Ellen asked, looking beyond him into the passageway.

'Staying over, she says. That's why I've got such a crook gut: I'm starving. So get along into that kitchen, girl.'

He turned back into the house. Ellen hesitated at the door. She had never been in the house alone with him when he was drunk.

'I wonder if I should come in for a while?' Miss Carvel said.

'I'll be all right,' Ellen said, although she felt scared.

Miss Carvel was thoughtful. 'I'm doing some more painting at the school tomorrow,' she said. 'I'll pop another book over for you—probably in the afternoon.'

'Yes, I'd like that,' Ellen said. 'I better go now, though. And thanks for taking me to the camp. It was wonderful.'

'I'm glad you had a chance to come, Ellen. I'll see you tomorrow.'

Ellen went into the house. In the kitchen, Mr Lewis was sitting at the table with a glass of beer, singing softly to himself.

He seemed not to notice Ellen, who hastily got his meal together, and placed it on the table.

'Will you need anything more?' she said. 'I'm a bit tired now.'

'Don't go running off yet, girl, there's the dishes to do when I've finished. Don't you want to keep me company?' He grinned unpleasantly at her, making Ellen shiver.

So she had to sit at the table, and watch him eat. He did so without looking at her, stopping only to fill his glass or to break into song. Ellen saw that his cheeks were inflamed. Now and again he spilt pieces of meat down his white shirt, or burped heavily. Then, suddenly, he pushed the plate aside, and laid his head down. In a moment he was asleep.

Ellen washed up the pans and dishes as quietly as she

could. She opened the kitchen door carefully, turned out the light, and tiptoed through the darkness to her hut. As she undressed, she thought happily about the brief moment of freedom she had found that afternoon.

In the morning Ellen woke earlier than usual. Remembering the night before, she got dressed quickly, and walked anxiously over to the house. To her relief, she found the kitchen empty. She walked through the house and up the stairs, and put her ear to the bedroom door. From inside came the sound of heavy snoring. She smiled, and crept back down to the kitchen.

How lovely, I'm free of them both for a bit, she thought. She made herself a cup of tea and some breakfast, fetched her book about Australia from the hut, and took them through to the front of the house.

She had never before had a chance to relax on the front verandah. She enjoyed sitting there in the shade of the wooden roof, taking in the sights and sounds of the street. A couple of women walked by, looked across at her, and passed on. She realized she had no idea who most of the people were who lived nearby. The mother of Grace's friend was the only person she had spoken to, and she always seemed to be in a hurry. Apart from the trips to the shops, it was like being a prisoner.

She opened her book, and looked for a section about the Aboriginals. Apart from two photos, there seemed to be very little on them. It said that they had come from the east some thirty thousand years ago, and that the ancestors of all the different tribes had set up their own areas, and that this time was called the Dreamtime. It also said that many of the Aboriginals had tried to get jobs in the towns, but that they had found it hard to change to a new way of life.

Ellen thought about those she had seen yesterday. Did they like being separate like that, having their own camp? The children seemed to be happy, to have a lot of freedom.

But wouldn't they get bored, always seeing the same people?

"Morning there!'

Ellen looked up, startled. A man was standing next to the mail box by the garden fence, holding an envelope.

'Oh, hello,' she replied.

'Are you Miss Ellen Duffy?'

'Yes.'

'Got a letter for you here.'

Ellen jumped up and ran to the gate. It must be from England, she thought excitedly.

'Oh, thank you,' she said, taking the letter.

'My pleasure,' the man said, looking at her curiously.

But as she walked back to the verandah, Ellen saw that the stamp was not English. She looked at the writing on the outside, and suddenly recognized it as Lizzie's. She tore open the envelope and read the letter.

Dear Ellen,

I'm sorry I haven't written before. I expect you realized Miss Reed forgot to give us our addresses, and that's why it took me a while to find out where you were.

I keep thinking about you and wondering how you're getting on. What is your family like, and also how about the school? The one here is quite boring, nobody likes it very much, and we have to do an awful lot of maths, which I'm no good at, do you remember? But at least it's not like the orphanage, and the teachers are all right, I suppose.

The worst bit is the family I'm with. Actually, Mrs Kerr is quite nice I think, but she's very nervous and quiet, and her husband is very bossy, and he's always complaining. So I have to work terribly hard. I always seem to be doing washing and ironing, and the house has to be cleaned all the time, and also I'm expected to weed the garden and things like that.

The trouble is, they've got three children, all a bit older than me, and they never have to do anything, and they're always having arguments and shouting at each other. The worst one is Eddie, and he's quite odd and creepy. At first he kept staring at me and following me about. Then last week he came into the kitchen when everyone was out, and tried to kiss me—it was awful, I just pushed him away. But since then he's tried twice more, and when I said I'd tell his dad, he said I better not, because otherwise he'd get me sent back to the orphanage. And I didn't know what to do then, I don't want to go back there. But I wonder how he got to know about the orphanage?

If he gets any worse, I've decided I will write to Miss Reed and ask if I can go to another house. I can remember her address from when we found it in Reverend Mother's desk.

I better stop now as I've got a lot of work to do, worse luck! Please write and tell me your news. Perhaps when it's holiday time we'll be able to meet again—I think my family are going away in July, so it would be lovely if we could.

     Love from Lizzie.

PS Have you heard from your mum or dad yet? I hope you have.

Ellen was pleased to hear from Lizzie. The mention of Miss Reed's address gave her a jolt. Of course, she thought, I can write to her and tell her how horrible and unkind Mr and Mrs Lewis are. Then she's bound to find me a better home.

She began to compose the letter in her head, and was doing this while cleaning the stove when Mrs Lewis returned.

'Are you still on that, girl?' she said, as soon as she was through the kitchen door. 'You were supposed to do that yesterday. Where's my husband?'

'I think he's upstairs,' Ellen replied.

'Take the baby then,' she said and, putting Charlie on the sofa, she left the room.

Grace was unusually quiet, and Charlie grizzled a little and sucked his thumb. Mrs Lewis returned to the room, scowling. 'He's disgusting,' she said. 'You'll need the mop and bucket again.'

It was the third time she had asked Ellen to clear up Mr Lewis's vomit. Now, suddenly, she couldn't stand the thought of doing it again.

'It's horrible, he should clear it up himself,' she said, trying to stay calm. She felt her face going red.

Mrs Lewis stared at her. 'What do you mean?'

'It's not fair.'

'You just do what I say, girl.'

'No, I won't. I'm not your slave.'

Mrs Lewis came up to her. 'How *dare* you answer me back!' she shouted. She slapped Ellen hard on the cheek, pushing her back on to the sofa, where she almost landed on Charlie. Both children started to cry.

'Now look what you've done!' Mrs Lewis screamed, coming towards the sofa. Ellen jumped up, ran round the table, opened the back door, and ran straight to her hut. She sat shaking on her bed, holding her cheek in pain. I hate her, I hate her, she sobbed. I shan't go on living here, I'll run away.

After a while her tears stopped. She looked up at the photograph above her bed. Usually it gave her hope, that one day the four of them would be together again, and happy, as they had been at that moment in the Welsh hills. But this time the picture made her feel lonelier than before. Suddenly nobody in it seemed to belong to her—they were just people in a picture.

I'm on my own, she thought. She remembered another day when she had the same overwhelming feeling: the day she first began school, and her terror then at having to leave Mum. Then she thought, I got through that all right, it was never as bad again. Perhaps this won't be either?

She knew now that nothing would get her out of the Lewis's house but what she did for herself, that it was all up

130

to her. But how was she going to escape? Then she remembered that Miss Carvel was going to drop in later. I have to tell *her* what's happened, *she'll* know what to do, she said to herself. But I can't just stay in here until then, I've got to go back to the house, otherwise I'll miss her. And I mustn't do that, I mustn't—even if it means having to go back and face that horrible woman! She picked the silver picture frame off the wall, and looked at her face in the shiny back of it. She'll know I've been crying, she thought; but I don't care any more.

And so she returned to the house. To her surprise, Mrs Lewis behaved as if nothing unusual had happened, although Ellen noticed she avoided looking at her. She said nothing more about cleaning up after Mr Lewis, but told Ellen to finish the stove and clean the rest of the kitchen, while she herself prepared the lunch. They worked in silence, while Grace played in the garden, and Charlie slept in the shade outside the back door.

Eventually Mr Lewis came downstairs. 'I think I'll just take a bit of a stroll before lunch,' he said, mumbling and looking at the floor. 'That all right?'

Mrs Lewis ignored him. He looked uncertainly at Ellen, and then edged out of the room. Ellen couldn't believe it was the same man who had been so loud and disgusting the night before.

As she gave Grace her bath, Ellen decided that Miss Carvel wasn't going to come after all. She felt let down. She had waited all afternoon, her hopes gradually fading as the big red sun fell lower in the sky. Several times she found a reason to go out into the front garden, where she would look down the street, hoping to see the dark blue car turning the corner.

'Just lay for the two of us,' Mrs Lewis said. That means he'll be coming back drunk again, Ellen thought. She decided she would go to bed as soon as possible after the meal. Her cheek was still hurting, and she felt more tired than usual.

They ate in silence, Mrs Lewis as usual reading a magazine. Then, as Ellen was clearing away, she opened the drawer of the kitchen table. 'By the way, your teacher friend called this morning,' she said. 'I told her you were out. She left this for you.' And she passed Ellen a small parcel.

Ellen didn't know whether to be angry or pleased. She realized she must have been crying in her hut when Miss Carvel had called, and that Mrs Lewis wouldn't have wanted her to see Ellen at that moment. On the other hand, Miss Carvel had kept her word, and Ellen had a new book to look at. She could hardly wait to finish the dishes.

As she reached the hut, and started to take the books out of the parcel, she heard shouting in the distance. The sun had almost set behind the hills outside the town, but as she went out into the garden again and looked through the broken fence, she saw three children running past a few yards away. One of them cried out, 'Hurry, we're going to miss it!'

Ellen felt the skin go cold all over her body. Suddenly she felt she had to follow them. She quickly climbed through the gap in the fence, and started to run along the backs of the houses, keeping the figures ahead of her in sight. They crossed the main street, and a few other people, caught up in the excitement, began to run, too. Then, as she came to a church on the corner of another street, Ellen suddenly knew where she was, and why she had come.

Her feet aching, her chest pounding, she stood and watched the flames pouring out of the windows of the school buildings. At one end, men with hoses were aiming jets of water at the fire. At the other, not yet reached by the flames, people were passing objects through the ground-floor windows.

Ellen remembered the night their neighbours' house in London had been hit by a rocket, killing the whole family.

She rushed forward to where people were standing, and pulled the sleeve of a woman at the front. 'Is anyone hurt, is anybody in there?' she cried out.

The woman's face looked hollow-cheeked in the light of the fire. 'We don't know yet, sweetie. Let's hope there isn't.'

Ellen stood there, unable to move, seeing nothing but Miss Carvel's face smiling at her through the flames.

Chapter 11

COMING TOGETHER

During the next few weeks the work on the farm was as hard and tiring as ever. The days seemed to get hotter, and Joe couldn't remember when he last saw a cloud. Sometimes the boys were allowed to work in the shade during the middle of the day, when the heat was even too much for Mr Temple. Otherwise there was no letting up. Joe still got his share of extra work and punishments. But at least now he had some hope to keep him going.

It was at this moment that Andy heard some news he'd been waiting for, and that Joe had secretly hoped would not come, at least not yet. Andy had told him he wanted to live in Australia, and was hoping to get a job on a sheep station. Now at last he was going to get his way, and would be leaving the school in six weeks' time. This made Joe long even more for some reply from England; he couldn't imagine what life would be like without Andy.

Each morning Joe looked out for the red handkerchief on Wal's windowsill—the signal they'd agreed on that a letter had arrived from England. One morning, as he was going out with a group to the building site, he saw it was there! He looked away and then back again: could it be real? Yes, there was no mistake. But then came the hard part: having to wait until the middle of the afternoon before he could get a break from work.

Luckily Wal was alone when Joe finally got to his office. Before Joe could say anything, Wal held up his hand.

'Now don't get too excited, mate,' he said. 'I've not had a letter yet.'

'Then why—' Joe began.

'Hold it, not so fast. Now listen here, Joe: do you trust me?'

'Yes, yes,' Joe said, impatiently.

'Right. And will you do what I say, and not ask me any questions about it, however strange it may seem?'

'All right,' Joe said, wondering what Wal meant.

'Good. Now listen to me carefully. Do you have a case for all the stuff you brought here?'

'Yes, I've got two, under my bed.'

'OK. When you go to bed tonight, make sure everything you've got is in them, and get into bed in what you're wearing now.'

'Why? What for?'

Wal smiled. 'Didn't I say no questions, mate?'

'Oh yes.'

'OK. Then, once you're in bed, listen for three knocks on the door. When you hear them, bring your cases and meet me outside, at the other end of the building. Be as quiet as you can, and don't tell anyone what you're doing or who you're meeting—not even Andy. That's hard, I know, but it's fairer on them. Understood?'

'Yes.'

'I can let you into one bonzer secret though, Joe,' he said, his voice excited now. 'This will certainly be your last day in this bugger of a place.'

As he walked back to his work, Joe tried to keep calm. His last day! So many questions came into his mind. How exactly would he get away? Where would Wal be taking him? Was he going to a different school? And supposing a letter arrived from England after he'd gone?

The afternoon dragged past slowly. At last work was over. As he and Andy were putting away the tools, Joe suddenly felt sad at leaving his friend. Then he had an idea.

'You know that swap you wanted,' he said.

'Which one?'

'Your penknife for my Chelsea badge.'

'Yes. What about it?'

'I don't mind doing it now.'

Andy looked at him in surprise. 'Are you sure?'

'Yes.'

'All right, then. Hey, wait till I tell Roy.'

Joe was first into the barn that evening, and quickly made sure that his possessions were packed. He put the Chelsea badge on Andy's pillow, climbed into bed, and pulled the blankets right up to his chin. Soon after, the other boys began drifting in from football.

'You're in bed early,' Andy said.

'I felt tired,' Joe replied.

'Hey thanks, Joe,' Andy said, seeing the badge. 'I'll give you the penknife tomorrow: Roy's got it at the moment. All right?'

'Yes, tomorrow will be OK,' Joe said. He watched his friend get ready for bed, and wondered if he would ever see him again.

''Night, Joe.'

''Night, Andy.'

Once the lights were out, Joe realized how tired he was. He had to fight hard to stay awake. Finally he heard three knocks on the door. He waited a moment, then slipped out of bed, put on his shoes, and took out the cases. He stole a last look at Andy sleeping, and moved quietly to the door. Opening it, he crept round the side of the building, and found Wal waiting for him.

'Well done, nipper,' Wal whispered. He took one of the cases from Joe. 'Now, I've got my car parked up on the bitumen. We'll have to go carefully: it's a fair cow of a night, with all this moonlight about. So just stick by me.'

They moved swiftly across the farm, covered most of the time by buildings or bushes. Wal signalled to Joe each time they had to dash fast across open space. Please don't see us, please don't see us, Joe said to himself at these moments. Finally they reached the safety of the large trees by the road, and there Joe saw the car.

'Starve the lizards!' Wal said, fighting to get his breath

back. 'I haven't run so fast for years, I'm really shagged. Thought I'd bust my gut. Anyway, that's the difficult part over.' He started the engine, and turned and smiled at Joe. 'You did well back there, mate. And now we'll head for my house. It's not far.'

Joe settled happily into the front seat. He didn't mind where he went, as long as he didn't ever, *ever* have to go back to the farm. As the car gained speed he looked across the moonlit landscape, and saw the two main houses, standing out cold and bright. Then they were hidden once more by the trees.

'But who did it?' Ellen asked. 'Haven't they found out yet?'

Miss Carvel sighed. 'Not yet. It might even have been an accident. Of course, there are stories: drunken Aboriginals is the most popular one at the moment.'

'But why should *they* want to do something like that?'

'There's a couple of Aboriginal children in the school. It's said one or two of the men in the camp don't approve of that.'

'Is that true?'

'I think it may be. But that doesn't mean they'd set light to the place. That's not the kind of thing they'd do.'

It was two days after the fire, and the first time Ellen had seen Miss Carvel since. That night she had eventually found out from one of the men fighting the fire that the school had been empty. After that she thought she had better get back to her hut. But it was only now, having bumped into Miss Carvel in the street, that she really believed she was safe.

'But what's going to happen about lessons?' Ellen asked.

'I'm afraid everyone's going to get a much longer holiday than they thought,' Miss Carvel replied. She laughed. 'Not that some of the children will be terribly upset by that. But I'm sorry about it for your sake.'

'So am I,' Ellen said, realizing what it meant.

137

Miss Carvel suddenly looked hard at her face. 'What's that mark on your cheek?' she said. 'It looks like some sort of bruise.'

'Yes, it is.'

'Oh dear. How did you get that?'

Ellen told her about the argument with Mrs Lewis, and how Mr Lewis was always getting drunk, and the way they both treated her just like a slave all the time.

Miss Carvel looked horrified. 'But why didn't you say this was going on?'

'I don't know,' Ellen said miserably. 'I suppose I was frightened to tell anyone.'

'Yes, of course. I can understand that.' Miss Carvel put her arm comfortingly round Ellen, and they walked slowly along the street together. 'Well, now you *have* told someone, this can't be allowed to go on. I'll get in touch straight away with the people who sent you here—what were they called?'

'The Fairlane Society.'

'Do you know where they are?'

'Yes. Lizzie and I learnt their address by heart when we were in the orphanage.'

'Good. I ought to write to them.'

'Oh, yes *please*,' Ellen said, relieved that someone was going to help her at last.

'Fine. But if there's any problem about finding somewhere else for you, I'll tell them you can move in with me for a while.'

'Oh, that would be lovely.'

'Meanwhile, I need to pay a visit to Mr and Mrs Lewis, and tell them what I'm doing.'

Ellen suddenly felt uneasy. 'Do you have to yet?' she said.

Miss Carvel stopped. 'Why do you say that?'

'It might be worse if they know I've told you everything. Couldn't we wait until Miss Reed writes back to you?'

'I see what you mean. All right, if you think you'll be

138

OK until then. I have another idea, though. Why don't I come up once a day and give you a lesson? I've got time on my hands until the school is ready again. That way, if either of them becomes violent again, just let me know, and I'll take you away on the spot.'

When Ellen told Mrs Lewis about the lessons, she could see she was not happy. But at least she didn't say Miss Carvel couldn't come. And that made Ellen feel safe—as well as giving her one hour a day to look forward to. It also had an effect on Mrs Lewis who, as if she knew her behaviour might be watched, treated Ellen less harshly, although she was still not friendly.

Ellen knew that Miss Carvel's letter and any reply had to rely on a mail plane for delivery. But after a month had passed she began to worry at not hearing anything. Then one evening when Miss Carvel arrived for her usual lesson, Ellen could see she was excited. They sat in the back garden as usual.

Miss Carvel made sure no one was looking, then passed Ellen a letter.

Ellen looked at the bottom of the letter, and saw it was from Miss Reed. Then she read the rest.

Dear Miss Carvel,

Thank you for your letter, which reached me last week.

We at the Society are naturally concerned at its contents, and are sure you have written it in good faith. However, it is only fair to point out that we have had a number of examples in recent years of children from England making claims about their foster parents which, on closer inspection, turn out to be exaggerated, sometimes wildly so.

In the circumstances, you will appreciate that we need to proceed cautiously. We would suggest that our inspector, Mr Jenkins, calls on Mr and Mrs Lewis when he is next in the area, and listens to their side of the story, and of course meets Ellen. Looking at his timetable, I think this is likely to be some time in the next six to eight weeks. I'm sure Mr

Jenkins—who is at present on the road—will be in touch with a firm date in the not too distant future.

I remain yours faithfully,
Emily Reed (Miss)

Ellen glanced anxiously at Miss Carvel. 'Does that mean they don't believe me?' she asked.

'It could do. But it also means nothing will happen for several weeks. Even then it's uncertain what they'll do.'

Ellen felt tears come to her eyes. The hope that had kept her going these last few weeks was draining away.

Miss Carvel came and squatted down next to her, her expression serious. She held Ellen's hand. 'Don't cry. There's no need to now. You've had quite enough of all this. Quick, go and pack your things. Then we'll go and tell Mrs Lewis you're leaving. And tomorrow I'll drive you straight to the Society's office—even if it does take us a couple of days to get there.'

Ellen was stunned. 'You mean I can leave?'

'I'd like to see anybody stop you!' Miss Carvel replied, her eyes flashing as she looked towards the house.

Ellen hurried to put her few possessions in her case, her heart beating in a way she had never felt it do before. She ran back up the garden path to join Miss Carvel. They found Mrs Lewis in the front room, sitting reading a magazine, with Charlie playing on the floor with some bricks. Ellen hung back in the doorway.

'Don't get up, Mrs Lewis, I won't keep you long,' Miss Carvel said, striding over to where she sat. 'Ellen told me some time ago about everything that's been going on here. I could hardly believe what she was telling me. How dare you treat a child like this!'

Ellen saw Mrs Lewis turn red. 'What do you mean? I don't know what you're talking about,' she said.

'Oh, yes, you do,' Miss Carvel replied, angrily. 'Slave labour I think it used to be called, not so long ago.'

Mrs Lewis rose from her chair. 'And who do you think you are, coming into my house and telling me what to do?'

'I'm just doing what anyone else would do in the same circumstances.'

'We'll see about that. My husband will be back from work shortly.'

Ellen saw Miss Carvel smile scornfully. 'Him? I think he's probably worse than you: a coward *and* a drunk.'

'Not such a coward down at your school the other night, was he?'

'What?'

'Shame about all those books and things, wasn't it?'

Miss Carvel stared at her. 'You mean—'

'I mean nothing.' She looked across at Ellen and noticed her suitcase. 'And where do you think you're going?'

'She's leaving right now,' Miss Carvel said. 'I've just had a reply to the letter I wrote to the Fairlane Society. I'm taking Ellen straight to their office, so she can tell them the full story herself. There'll be no more children coming here, Mrs Lewis, you can be sure of that.' She walked to the door, then turned again. 'And when I get back, I'll pass on what you've just told me to the police.'

As they left the room, Ellen saw Mrs Lewis put her hands to her head. While the two women had been talking, she had been afraid that Mrs Lewis might suddenly try to stop Miss Carvel from taking her away. Now she knew she was safe, she found she couldn't stop shaking.

In the garden, Grace was playing with some earth. She'll be the only thing I'll miss about this place, Ellen thought. She went up to her, gave her a quick hug, and then walked out to join Miss Carvel. She was free at last.

'Here we are, mate: Wal's palace.'

Joe looked through the car window. He saw the outline of a single small building, with lighted windows either side of a darkened porch.

'The door's open: make yourself at home, Joe,' Wal said. 'I'll park the car round the back and bring your cases through.'

Joe got out, and looked about him. The moon had disappeared, but he saw other lights not far off, the shapes of houses all around. The night felt calm and warm as he walked the short distance to Wal's. As he drew near the house, he saw someone open the door and stand in the half-lit porch. He stopped, uncertain suddenly, but wanting to go on.

'Joe?'

The voice sounded odd, it seemed to come from another time. Someone's playing a trick on me, Joe thought. Then he heard it again.

'It's me, Joe. It's Mum.'

The figure came into the light. And then he knew it was no trick. He stood there awkwardly, not knowing what to say. Then she ran to him, and he threw his arms around her waist, felt her hands stroking his hair and face. They stayed like that for a while, until she spoke again.

'Can you forgive me, Joe, can you? For letting all this happen?'

He knew she was crying, but he didn't want to look.

'Why are you here?' he said, not understanding.

'Why? Because I've come to fetch you, Joe, to take you back home.'

He listened to the word for a long time. Home. Then he woke up, and pulled away from her.

'Dad and Ellen!—are they here, too?'

Mum took his hand. They started to walk back to the house. 'No, they're not,' she said. 'Dad's in England—but he's much better now. He'll be back at work in a few weeks' time.' She stopped, and looked down at Joe. 'I don't know where Ellen is exactly. But we'll find her soon enough, Joe. Wal has the society's address.'

Joe held her hand tightly until they reached the house, where they found Wal waiting for them. At last, in the light, Joe could see Mum properly. He noticed at once that her hair was longer, and that she was wearing ear-rings, which he had never seen her do before. But nothing about her had really changed: she still looked at him in that anxious way he had got used to, a tiny frown crossing her small, oval face.

He wanted to ask her lots of questions, but just then Wal interrupted. 'Fair old surprise, eh, sport?' he said, grinning broadly. He beat his fist into the palm of his other hand. 'I can't wait to see Piggot's face in the morning.'

Joe nodded. But his mind was too full of tonight to think about tomorrow.

The little waiting-room was hot and sticky, even with the fan running in the corner. Ellen found it hard to keep still. Why were they taking so long? Didn't Miss Reed believe what Miss Carvel was telling her?

On the wall opposite she noticed several photographs. She got up and went over to look. They were all of groups of children, with dates and places written underneath— some going back twenty years, she noticed. Then she saw that one was of a group from Our Lady of the Assumption. The girls were wearing the same uniforms as she and Lizzie had. Ellen studied their faces. They looked happy and cheerful, she thought. But what if someone had come to take our picture there, would Lizzie and I have been smiling too? Yes, that's what the Sisters would have told us to do.

She returned to her seat, suddenly tired. The journey with Miss Carvel had been a hard one. The country they passed through had no longer interested her. Flat, empty and dusty, it seemed quite different from how it had looked from the air. She had spent much of the time asleep. Occasionally she and Miss Carvel had sung songs or played word games, but soon she had tired of this, too. All she had wanted was to arrive.

At last Miss Reed and Miss Carvel came out of the office. Miss Carvel came and sat next to her.

'Well, Miss Duffy, you seem to have had rather bad

luck,' Miss Reed began. 'This is most unusual, of course, as I was explaining to Miss Carvel. We take great care in our choice of family. But just occasionally something can go wrong.'

'Rather badly wrong in this case,' Miss Carvel said sharply. 'I only hope Ellen's brother has been more lucky.'

'Oh, have you found out where he is?' Ellen said, her voice rising with excitement. 'Is he all right?'

'Certainly he is,' Miss Reed said, rather coldly. 'He's at one of the better farm schools, about a hundred miles from here. We have very good reports of it.'

'Can I visit him, then?' Ellen said quickly.

'First things first. My priority is to find you an alternative place to live.'

'But I want to see Joe!'

'I'm sure we can arrange that before too long. Meanwhile, there is a family in this town who regularly take in our girls. They have a vacancy at the moment; their last girl has just got a job up in the north. I've arranged for you to meet them tomorrow morning. And for tonight we can get you a room in the hotel here.' She paused. 'And also for Miss Carvel, at her suggestion.'

'Yes, Ellen: I want to stay on, just to see that you're all right. And I'm sure, in the circumstances, Miss Reed won't mind if I come with you tomorrow, to see your new family.'

Miss Reed frowned. 'Well, I don't know—'she began.

'In the circumstances,' Miss Carvel broke in, firmly.

'I see. Well, perhaps we *can* arrange that, though it's not, of course, normal practice.' Miss Reed stood up abruptly. 'And now I must get back to work. I will see you at ten tomorrow.'

Joe remembered that other journey, and how lost and upset he had been. This time everything was different. As the train steamed steadily through the plains and small towns, he was able to look properly at the places they were going through, and wonder at the wide, lonely land he had been trapped in for so long.

After a while, he turned back from the scene outside, to check that Mum was still sitting opposite. He had done this several times during the journey, as if she might vanish if he looked away for too long. This time she had closed her eyes, and her head was tilted back against the seat. He looked at her pale face, caught in the fierce morning sun. She seems older than before, he thought suddenly. He leaned over and prodded her awake.

'Oh, was I asleep?' She blinked for a moment, smiled at him, and looked at her watch. 'Only another ten minutes, Joe.'

Joe became anxious. 'They won't try and keep me there, will they?' he asked.

'Oh no, they have no right to do that, I promise you, Joe,' Mum replied, combing her hair in a small mirror.

'But what if your letter hasn't arrived.'

'That won't matter. I shall tell them about the farm myself.'

Soon they arrived at the station. A tall, blond man helped them with their cases, and they climbed down on to the platform, standing for a moment in the welcome shade of the train.

Several other people were getting off, too. Joe watched another man get out from the next carriage, and a woman come across and shake hands with him. In the distance a girl was waving, while on a seat nearer to them two boys were arguing in high-pitched voices. He saw the girl running in their direction, disappearing for a moment behind the couple, then swerving into sight again, faster than before. A few yards away she stopped—and Joe saw that it was Ellen.

No one moved or spoke. Then Ellen said: 'I *hoped* you'd be on this train.'

Joe looked up at Mum, and saw her bite her lip. Then she

held out her arms to both of them, and the three of them came together in a long embrace.

After a while, Joe became aware of someone watching them. He turned, and saw a tall, dark-haired young woman looking at them, smiling.

'What do you want?' Joe said, without thinking.

Ellen turned round, too. 'Oh, Mum, this is Miss Carvel, she helped me to escape, and then she brought me all the way here in her car, and—'

'Escape from what, Ellen?'

Ellen stopped, too excited to think straight. Miss Carvel came forward. 'Hello, Mrs Duffy, hello, Joe: I'm *so* pleased you've found us,' she said.

'You can imagine what *I* feel,' Mum said, shaking Miss Carvel's hand warmly. 'Whatever you have done for Ellen, I thank you a thousand times.'

'There's an awful lot to tell you. But I expect right now you just want to be alone with your children?'

Mum looked at the two of them happily. Then her face became solemn. 'What I want most of all is to find out what this so-called children's welfare society thinks it's playing at. Do you know the way to their office?'

'Yes, we just came from there,' Miss Carvel replied. 'Miss Reed got your letter this morning.'

'Then let's go back now, and get it over with,' Mum said firmly. 'This Miss Reed and her gang have an awful lot to answer for.'

Ellen and Joe had agreed they would wait until the land had disappeared from sight before saying anything. As they stood at the ship's rail, they saw the thin grey strip of Australia, still just visible right out on the horizon, growing fainter every moment.

In the time between finding Mum and Joe, and the day of their departure, Ellen had tried several times to find the right words. But Mum had been so busy—with long, angry meetings with Miss Reed, talking to Miss Carvel, booking their voyage, sorting out passports—that the right moment had never come. Now they had her to themselves, and Ellen knew she had to have an answer.

'Look, it's gone!' Joe called out suddenly.

'What's gone, Joe?' Mum said, from her deck-chair a few yards away.

'The land has. I can only see water now.'

She laughed. 'You'd better get used to that for the next six weeks.'

Joe looked at Ellen. She nodded. They moved across to where Mum was sitting, her eyes closed, the breeze rippling her hair.

'Mum,' Ellen began.

'Mmmm?'

'Can we ask you something?'

'Of course, love.'

Ellen hesitated, then spoke in a rush. 'When we get back to London, where are you going to live?'

Mum opened her eyes slowly. 'Where am I going to live?' She looked out across the sea. 'No, you're right. We haven't discussed it at all, have we? And really I should have asked you both first, asked you before anyone else.'

'Asked us what, Mum?' Ellen said.

Mum rose, and joined them at the rail. 'You know, I've acted very selfishly these last few months. All this wouldn't have happened to you if I had been at home when you needed me. Anyway, I had a long talk with Dad before I left England. He's been very understanding. He says he'd like me to come home again.'

There was a short silence. 'What do you think of that idea?' she asked anxiously.

Ellen clutched her arm. 'Oh yes, Mum, that's what *we* want too. Don't we, Joe?'

Joe remembered the nights when he had lain in bed, listening to raised voices. He thought, too, of other voices and sounds he had heard more recently, at the farm school.

'But will you still shout at Dad?' he said.

Mum waited before she spoke. 'I'll try not to, I'll try very hard. But I can't make any promises. Do you understand that, Joe?'

'Yes,' Joe said, even though he didn't.

Ellen felt her body relax. So they would have a home again, and be able to get back to normal. She hugged Mum, who smiled, and then looked serious again.

'Ellen,' she said, holding her away at arm's length.

'Yes.'

'There's one other thing. Perhaps I should have told you before. It's about Lizzie.'

'Lizzie! Oh, did you find out if she's all right? Will she be able to come back to England too?'

'I don't know, love. You see, Miss Reed managed to get through on the phone. Apparently . . . it seems that she's run away.'

'Run away? Where to?' Ellen said, taken aback.

'No one knows. She just disappeared one morning, without even taking any of her things.'

'Oh, poor Lizzie,' Ellen said, half to herself. 'But where will she go?'

'I don't really know, love,' Mum replied.

Ellen stood for a moment, trying to imagine where Lizzie might be now. But all she could see in her mind was the hard, hot, unforgiving landscape that they were now leaving behind.

'Would you mind if I went for a walk, Mum?' she said finally.

'Of course not,' Mum replied.

'Will you come, Joe?'

Joe looked up at her. 'All right,' he said.

As the two of them walked slowly towards the front of the ship, Ellen looked up, and noticed some gulls beginning to circle above them, as they headed towards home.